Copyright © 2020 by Ha

The characters and events portrayed in this book
real persons, living or dead, is coincidental and 1

No part of this book may be reproduced, or stored in a retrieval system, or transmitted in any form or by any means, electronic, mechanical, photocopying, recording, or otherwise, without express written permission of the publisher.

ISBN: 9798590259663

Cover art by Cath Grace Designs

Other books by Haley Cass

Those Who Wait

When You Least Expect It

Better Than Expected

In the Long Run

Down to A Science

On the Same Page

Dedication & Acknowledgements

Honestly, the only dedication and acknowledgement that needs to be made for *Forever and A Day* is to the readers.

I never once imagined that you would connect with Charlotte and Sutton so much as a couple, as much as I have. These two characters live in my mind so completely ever since writing them for the first time.

But *Those Who Wait* became what it has become because of every reader who took in that 600 page romance and wanted even more time with those women.

So, this is for all of you. I hope you enjoy it.

||*Huffpost*||

Feature: How Charlotte Thompson is Becoming the New Face of Politics
March 22, 2020

Thompson nabbed the House of Representatives seat vacated eight months ago by the late John Kelvin in a close race last Tuesday. After leading Naomi Young in polls by at least twenty percent for the duration of the election, Thompson's lead fell to less than ten percent as she came out as a lesbian only ten days prior.

Thompson, 28, is now the youngest openly gay member of Congress and she's here to make a mark.

When questioned about her opponent, Naomi Young, Thompson spoke candidly.

"I haven't gotten into this life to mince words, like many of my peers have. Naomi Young made a point to threaten revealing my sexuality throughout this election. People like that have no business working in the government, where they would continue to work in the favor of oppression. I am a lesbian. And I'm not ashamed. And I'm going to fight for what's right as long as I'm in a position to do so."

Part 1

Since coming out as a lesbian so early in her career had never been *the plan*, Charlotte hadn't really known much of what to expect. Ever since the interview came out six months ago, she'd been on a learning curve.

Luckily, she'd always been a fast learner.

The fact that she'd still beat Naomi – even with her polling numbers taking a disheartening but unsurprising dip – had been shocking and elating, and it allowed her enough breathing room to have hope that she still could have her future intact.

One of the biggest changes was the publicity.

Going from a relatively faceless rising name in the New York City's Mayoral office to the House of Representatives would have been a decent shift into the public light no matter what. But since she'd done it while being an out lesbian, her media exposure was easily triple what most others experienced.

It wasn't as though paparazzi were chasing her through the streets – thankfully – but the publicity was extreme. Her face and name remained on news headlines longer than was typical, she was featured in handfuls gossip magazines even, but she'd done her best to take that in stride.

At the end of the day, she'd achieved what she'd set out to do. Doing more interviews and photoshoots and getting her name out there more wasn't necessarily a bad thing.

She just had to make the best of it.

The backlash, with her dropping polling numbers and the critical pieces that cropped up against her, were . . . unpleasant. To say the least. Anxiety-inducing to say the most, but she didn't let herself get that far. At times she couldn't quite let it all go as easily as she wished she could, but at the very least it was all entirely predictable.

She'd expected a backlash.

Opposite of that, however, had been the positive side that she hadn't quite ever let herself consider. The new allies and connections she'd gotten in her own world, and especially the people who'd reached out to her and used words like inspiring, powerful, moving. The people who'd thanked her for being the next step forward. The people who, in their words, she represented.

The influx of followers on all of her social medias alone was – overwhelmingly supportive. Almost alarmingly so.

She tried to not delve into those, either.

All in all, though, she didn't regret it. How could she? No, it wasn't her plan, but plans sometimes had to change.

The last six months had been an adjustment. A nerve-wracking, relatively public adjustment that at first had been terrifying but luckily Charlotte had always managed to be adaptable.

And in the place of not being *adaptable* at every turn, she was able to save face.

Everything was turning out to be *okay* as the dust had finally started to settle. That alone was better than she'd ever imagined.

The biggest change of all though, was being with Sutton.

Sutton, her official girlfriend.

Sutton, who had officially been in Rome for one hundred and thirty-three days – and counting, now that she'd gotten the offer to extend her internship for the additional three months.

Never in her life had she navigated this aspect of her life. Had to navigate being in a *relationship*, let alone juggling a relationship where her girlfriend was halfway around the world.

She'd also never made use of her vacation time since she'd worked in public office. Not once in over six years had she taken more than the mandated holidays off, and yet –

"I still can't believe you're here," Sutton breathed out, her voice just a bit hoarse and lazy still. Charlotte couldn't stop herself from smiling into Sutton's back as she continued planting slow kisses across the top of her back.

"Believe it," she murmured, tossing her hair over her shoulder and looking at the clock next to the bed. "At least for the next thirty-two hours."

She sat up on her knees taking in with a just barely sated hunger all of Sutton's soft skin on display, as she lay completely naked underneath her. All of that glorious long red hair was swept to the side, mussed and tangled from the night they'd spent in bed together after Charlotte had arrived.

Her lips quirked up a bit into a smirk and she brushed her fingers over the dark spot she'd sucked into the juncture where Sutton's neck and shoulder met, loving how she could see the way Sutton shivered at it.

The utterly self-indulgent satisfied feeling that slid through her with the fact that Sutton was *her girlfriend*, that they'd made it over those initial hurdles coupled with the fact that Sutton was still so completely responsive to her touch was on the precipice of familiar and novel. She reveled in it.

"I wish it was for longer." Sutton's voice was slightly muffled as she arched her back against Charlotte's hands.

She traced her fingers along the muscles there, biting her lip at the longing in Sutton's voice, because she felt it too. The want for more time together that was only hushed with the knowledge that this distance was temporary.

"I know, believe me. I'm sorry, darling, but these few days I have off have already killed my schedule," her voice was soft and full of remorse, because she *did* wish there was more time for them right now, to be together in the same place.

She was well aware that if her job and schedule weren't the way it was, taking a few more days off to stay in Rome wouldn't be out of the question. A soft pang of guilt and the stresses she still carried about the future brought her slowly exploring hands to a pause.

She shook her head to push those thoughts away. Worries about the future would be normal in any relationship, she not only assured herself but had been assured by Sutton multiple times after sharing these feelings with her. They would just have to figure things out as they came and there were some things that couldn't be mapped out. She had to be okay with that.

She bent down, sliding her hands along Sutton's sides, to press her lips against the nape of her neck. The feeling of Sutton against her, the smell of her shampoo that lingered in her hair, was enough to help calm her ever-present thoughts about the future.

There was no way she was going to waste the precious little time she had here on that. Not when they were secluded in a room with just the two of them, away from everything and everyone.

She could *feel* Sutton melt even more into the mattress, even before she shook her head. "No, it's not – Charlotte, you have so much to do, and you took time off to come here. That's . . . you're so perfect." Her tone was dreamy.

It made Charlotte grin with the rush of pride, feeling the need to live up to that tone.

"Mm, I do try. You're no slouch in the busy department, either, over here making a name for yourself, and trying to squeeze those of us back home in when you can," she teased, stroking her fingers down, just over the sides of Sutton's chest, knowing the way she would shudder lightly from it.

Sutton scoffed, even as her heart skipped a beat that Charlotte could feel it from where her lips pressed against her shoulder blade.

"I've heard – *hmm* –" She broke off in a light hum as Charlotte pushed herself back up and stroked up her spine in a light massage.

She'd arrived at Sutton's apartment from the airport just in time for Sutton to get out of her internship and she hadn't been able to stop touching her since. She'd mapped just about every inch of her body at this point, she thought, as she watched her own hands slide over Sutton's shoulders.

"I've heard," Sutton started again. "From a little bird, that you've even had dinner with Regan on her late nights at the café," her voice was a mixture between giggling and utter relaxation, before she turned her head enough to look at Charlotte over her shoulder, blue eyes sparkling in mirth. "You must *really* miss me back home if you and Regan are becoming dinner buddies."

Narrowing her eyes, she scratched down her spine, enjoying the way Sutton squealed at the change of motion. She tried to focus on that instead of the embarrassment that settled low in her stomach. "Don't mock; you've left us both in quite the lurch."

She and Regan *had* caught the occasional dinner together as of late. She wouldn't yet classify them as friends, but they were headed in that direction. Probably. It wasn't something she'd sought out to do but it was happening anyway, especially in light of both of them missing Sutton.

She pursed her lips and huffed out a breath. "Besides, I figure it's better if we resolve any remaining issues now. Get that all out of the way."

Not that they had many at this point. Her mortifying breakdown and declaration of loving Sutton, post her coming out interview when Regan had ultimately offered her help to get Charlotte into the wedding six months ago, had certainly helped them overcome most of their barriers.

"Yeah?" Sutton's head, that had previously been resting on the pillow while Charlotte had settled on top of her, popped up while a tentative, hopeful tone edged in her voice.

"Yes, well, you won't be here away from us forever." She reached out to push Sutton's hair over her shoulder as it had moved with her and splayed over her back, before she rose back up to her knees in preparation to push herself back into the spot next to Sutton on the mattress.

Who made a sound in the back of her throat in protest as Charlotte moved to shift off of her and she paused. Sutton instead maneuvered and flipped onto her back, looking up at her from the pillow.

Those blue eyes were tired but bright, the smile on her lips was lazy and sated, and she reached out to take Charlotte's hands with hers, their fingers easily threading together. She settled comfortably straddling Sutton's hips, flexing her fingers in the hands holding hers, and let her eyes drift closed for a moment.

Just to feel it all. She'd needed this.

They'd had barely a month together back home before Sutton had gone away for her internship, and that month had been so incredibly hectic. It had been Charlotte's busiest month of her career so far, tying up all loose ends and starting her new responsibilities and new –impossibly longer – hours.

Not to mention the media circus that she'd been trying to sidestep as much as she could.

Sutton had to finish all of her graduate school tasks and had spent another week and a half of that time with her family. They'd both agreed to not throw this – this warm, lovely, sparkling but incredibly *new* – relationship into the public fire that had only turned from simmer to boil as Sutton had left for Rome.

She had thought, apparently wildly incorrectly – and god knew how much she hated being wildly incorrect – that Sutton doing her internship wouldn't be the worst thing with the timing of it all.

She'd thought that she'd focus on her job and by the time Sutton came back from Rome she would have it and the newfound publicity well in hand. Not that she'd *wanted* Sutton to not be there with her, but she'd figured it wouldn't be terribly difficult to put the majority of her focus on other things while they were apart. That it would be a good time to regroup and fall more into a routine.

Loathe as she was to admit it, she'd been very wrong.

Of course, they video chatted regularly – every Saturday without fail, as it was Sutton's guaranteed day off even if her schedule got shifted around, and whenever else they could fit it in. They texted every day. They *communicated*, despite the six-hour time difference and both of their busy schedules, all of the time.

Logically, things should be easier without Sutton back in New York. She should have more time to focus on work and for their relationship to not be dragged into public speculation while she was also still dealing with the fallout of coming out.

But it wasn't easier at all.

Because in spite of still talking to Sutton every day, she *missed* her. She wished she could have their coffee dates or movie nights or even just come home to her. It was almost scary, how intense this want for Sutton was.

And because of a whole jumble of those feelings, she'd found herself booking a flight to Rome for a short trip. Just to reaffirm… all of this. For her to know that everything they had was still there and real.

They'd *reaffirmed* that this was most certainly still here and real six times in the last twelve hours; her body was still tingling with it.

"Should I always plan on you chasing me whenever I go away?" Sutton spoke softly, a teasing lilt in her voice to bring Charlotte out of her thoughts. But there was also a genuine wonder there, a soft insecurity.

"I think we've well established that I'm exceptional in seeking you out," she murmured. She could hear the affection in her voice mirroring what was lacing through her veins.

It should be mortifying, really, that she felt this deep, true affirmation inside of her – *yes*. She *would* chase after Sutton whenever she left, while they were together. Never in her life had she thought she would be someone who would take days off of work to fly literally across the world for matters of the heart. And yet –

The way Sutton's smile widened, brightened, her eyes crinkling with sheer happiness at her answer shredded any negative feelings she could have at that truth.

Charlotte quirked her head to the side, shifting her hips a bit to rock forward onto Sutton. "Should I always plan on you calling in sick when I arrive?"

"I – you – we were up all night!" Sutton's voice fell to a hush, as it had earlier when she'd called in faking sick to her supervisor. As though someone from her internship was going to pop up from the corner of the small rented apartment to catch her faking.

Charlotte found it equal parts adorable and hilarious, and she couldn't help but laugh even as she nodded. "We were. Perhaps you should have been the responsible person here and put a stop to it."

She let go of Sutton's hands and braced her own on the pillow on either side of Sutton's head as she ducked down. Her breath caught in her throat as her bare chest pressed against Sutton's, the arousal that hadn't fully been sated stirring again as she nuzzled Sutton's jaw, and felt her catch and hold a breath.

"I," she released it on a long shudder, her nipples hard and pressing into Charlotte's chest. "I don't think you're one to talk about res-responsibility," Sutton stuttered as she rocked her hips down against her and nipped at her neck.

It was so incredibly heady, this hunger for Sutton. She was still wet for her and wanting her all over again. And the fact that she could feel Sutton's pulse scrambling against her lips as she pressed a kiss to her neck just made it feel even headier.

"On the contrary; I'm very responsible," she whispered. "Or do you not know who you're talking to?" She scratched down Sutton's side, just enough to make her arch under her as she leaned back down. She sighed as she felt Sutton's hands move to grip her thighs.

And then she squealed as she was flipped onto her back, a rush going through her as it always did when Sutton surprised her in bed. Especially when Sutton surprised her and slid her hands down to Charlotte's wrists to hold them to the bed, with *that* glint in her eye.

"I know just who you are, Congresswoman Thompson," she whispered as she leaned down, stopping just a whisper before their mouths connected.

The wanting inside of her that was already so strong only got more intense as *Congresswoman Thompson* washed over her. She couldn't have stopped herself from leaning up and capturing Sutton's lips with hers even if she'd wanted to.

Sutton pressed her hips against Charlotte, grinding into her and she groaned low in her throat at the pressure, knowing Sutton could feel just how wet she was all over again.

She bit at Sutton's bottom lip, tugging it between her teeth as she brought her thighs up to wrap around Sutton's waist.

"God, I don't think you saying that will ever get old," she managed to get out, her breath already coming shorter as she rolled her hips up against Sutton.

She didn't think most things Sutton made her feel would ever get old and that alone was still a new, incredible feeling. It made something inside of her twist and dip low in her stomach, her heart skip a beat, and it was unfamiliar but *good*.

"We should probably make the most of that while you're here, then," Sutton panted into her mouth, her warm breath washing over Charlotte's jaw as she scratched her fingers lightly down Charlotte's sides, goosebumps popping up in their wake.

As Sutton's teeth nipped at the side of her breast, she groaned. "We definitely should."

One of her hands fisted into Sutton's hair as she continued her descent down her body; god, they had so much to take advantage of.

***

E!News

Love is in full bloom

After months of speculation about **Charlotte Thompson**'s love life and relationship status, her "more than a friend" **Sutton Spencer** has resurfaced. Spencer, pictured left, was seen leaving Thompson's apartment early this morning after having dropped off the radar shortly after Thompson's election last March, during which the two were notably linked.

Sorry ladies, but it appears Thompson is once again off the market. The reunited couple was spotted looking pretty cozy while out to dinner in midtown last night.

"They were never ****ing broken up," an insider says.

Life is looking good for the Congresswoman these days and we are positively jealous. Are you rooting for them to make it? Let us know in the comments!

1/13/21

Part 2

Sutton had only been back from her internship for a few days, but everything had hit the ground running, almost as if she hadn't even left.

Seven months in another country had been . . . incredible. Exciting, exhausting at times, especially with the occasional late nights she'd pulled to stay up to talk to her family, friends, and Charlotte. She'd learned so much, seen some of the oldest and most incredible literature and art in the world, and made new connections.

But she'd missed home. She'd missed watching her shows and having dinner with Regan, had missed phone and video calls with her family that came through clearly. And she'd really, really missed Charlotte.

While she didn't regret going on the internship or the experience in the least, she was happy to be back.

Even if everything *was* absolutely insane.

And not necessarily in the good kind of way, if that was any sort of a thing. She rolled her eyes at herself, unable to stop fidgeting from where she stood in the sitting room outside of the office. Elizabeth Thompson's office on the top floor of the Thompson Foundation.

The office that she'd been *summoned* to. Quite literally summoned. Which was, well, it was kind of terrifying. She wasn't sure if the fact that she was dating Elizabeth Thompson's granddaughter was supposed to make it less anxiety inducing, but it didn't.

God. It was only noon and today already felt like it lasted for a week.

She'd woken up early, even earlier than Charlotte's alarm, with anticipation crawling through her because she had an interview. An actual, real interview at Hunter College to work as their new adjunct literature professor. Dr. Martin had recommended it to her, sending her the application during the last month of her internship.

Despite his belief that she would get the job, especially as she'd worked for him before and he was in line to become the next chair of the department, it was – well, nerve-wracking.

But it had gone well. Well enough that as she'd left the interview, she'd felt fairly confident.

She didn't even have a moment afterwards to really reflect on it, though, because as soon as she'd checked her phone, she'd seen that there had been sixty-one texts and twelve missed calls.

The dread that shot through her, thinking that someone she cared about had been hurt – or worse – had been overwhelming. And then that faded into an entirely different but still overwhelming feeling when she'd realized exactly what the subject of those messages was.

Her relationship.

More aptly: her relationship being made entirely public, with pictures of her splashed all over gossip websites.

She'd spent the previous night at Charlotte's for the first time since she'd arrived home a few days ago, and she'd had absolutely no idea that there'd been a member of the paparazzi nearby. How could she have known? Whoever it was snapped a handful of pictures of her, most notably as she'd given Charlotte's doorman a small smile on her way out and had connected her with having dinner with Charlotte the night before.

And had also made the connection that she'd been Charlotte's photo companion during her election, too.

The articles had stopped her short, the world falling away, as she saw her own face splashed with commentary and speculation. It seemed almost everyone she'd ever met had seen it and wanted to comment on it.

While she and Charlotte had been together for the very short time before her internship, they'd kept their relationship as private as possible. Not only for

Sutton's sake, because she *hadn't* felt comfortable with all of that attention on her.

But because at the time, she'd been a little worried that it would be too much pressure for Charlotte. Having just come out, to then also have the speculation on *them*.

Then she'd been away in Rome and this was just – it was so new.

Of course, she'd been in pictures with Charlotte before. But before the election had happened, she was Charlotte Thompson's relatively nameless friend. But given how Charlotte's popularity and buzz had skyrocketed in the last eight months, she guessed this wasn't exactly a surprise.

She just hadn't been expecting it. She hadn't even thought about it, really, because it seemed so far removed from her life.

She definitely hadn't been prepared for the comments section on the article she'd read. She only scrolled a little bit, but it was enough. Some had been encouraging and they made her feel a little calmer. Some had been complimentary toward her, which was nice, if a little – too much. Some had been far too lewd and had turned her stomach. Some had been, uh, unfavorable, and those had been what made her quickly exit out of it all.

Sutton had been entirely thrown, especially as she'd walked toward the subway and *felt* that there were eyes on her. That some of the people talking as she'd passed were talking about her.

And then she'd gotten a call from a number that was entirely unfamiliar, and of course hadn't answered it, given this shock of publicity. But the voicemail that had been left –

"Miss Spencer, I'm calling on behalf of Elizabeth Thompson. She would like to have a meeting with you at your earliest possible convenience; I've given your name for clearance to the top floor offices at the Thompson Foundation for the rest of the afternoon. If you cannot make it today, please call this number back to reschedule."

So, that hadn't made her feel any less anxious, because why did Elizabeth Thompson want to see her enough to have her called to her office in the middle of what Sutton was sure was a busy day?

And she knew Charlotte didn't know about this because Charlotte had been one of her missed calls and texts, apologizing for this media storm and sounding stressed, wanting to talk about it all later.

Which, hell, also didn't make her feel like this was any less surreal.

Not that she had the same worries now that she did before – that Charlotte could be somehow scared away from giving them a try. Because, with a little warm feeling in her stomach that she latched onto, the last months had been so affirming for them.

Like the fact that Charlotte always made time for her. That she was always beaming whenever Sutton told her about her accomplishments. Like the fact that she didn't ever miss a chance to tell Sutton that she loved her.

"Miss Spencer? Mrs. Thompson will see you now," one of the secretaries, the one farthest from the double doors that lead into what she presumed was Elizabeth Thompson's office, gave her a slight smile, before answering another phone call.

Sutton wiped her palms on her thighs and channeled both of her parents' calmness the best she could, as she pushed the door open slowly.

Elizabeth Thompson sat behind her desk as she had her hands interlinked in front of her, giving Sutton an expectant look the moment she walked through the door.

"Shut that behind you." She gave a sharp nod and Sutton hurried to do as she said, even as the older woman was already speaking, "I'm glad you could come in so soon after receiving my call; I appreciate expediency."

As the door clicked closed quietly, Sutton took a moment there with her hand on the knob to take a deep breath, slowly exhaling and rubbing her hand over her stomach to quell the unease there before she turned. "Of course! I had a few free hours." She turned to face her, eyebrows drawing together. "I just – I'm not exactly sure what you called me here for. Ma'am."

She almost cringed at herself for *that*, but stopped herself in time, as she made her way to the chair opposite the desk.

But what exactly was she supposed to say to Elizabeth Thompson? The thought of it sent nerves jangling through her; she knew, logically, how she was supposed to formally address politicians in any stature, retired or not; given the nature of her father's profession, she couldn't even remember when she'd learned the proper manners and terms to use.

But she'd never had this kind of situation. With the former President giving her a critically contemplative look. Former President, first female President, who also happened to be her girlfriend's idolized grandmother. Who she'd only met her once before and, well, she hadn't seemed to like her all that much.

Elizabeth scoffed. "Is that why in the hell you look so afraid?" She didn't seem like she was waiting for an answer, not that Sutton could have really given one to her that didn't sound probably really dumb. "Don't worry, this won't take much of your time. I have the Chancellor of Germany on line two."

Sutton blinked at her. "Um. Okay." She crossed her legs, linking her hands over her knees to force herself to stop fidgeting. With a deep breath, she tilted her head and confessed. "I'm confused."

Elizabeth didn't make her wait with any pleasantries. "I'm going to assume you're not entirely oblivious and that you've realized your relationship with my granddaughter is now very public."

The words were cut and dry, almost harsh in the effective tone they were delivered in, and she felt herself flush. "Of course. I saw it earlier –"

"I know my granddaughter never foresaw the time coming where she would fall in love," Elizabeth effectively cut her off, leaning forward in her desk chair and holding eye contact with Sutton. "But I've always wondered if this time would come and how exactly to prepare for it. I know my Charlotte; if she would fall for someone hard enough to put her career in jeopardy," she paused, giving Sutton a *look* that made her muscles tense. "There would be no talking her into reason. So I'm prepared to be the voice of reason for her."

Sutton's spine drew up straight, shoulders back, almost defensively. Much like the way, she realized a moment after she did it, Charlotte did when she felt threatened or vulnerable and was hiding it.

"I don't know what you mean by that," her voice was steady, though, and she was proud of that. Even as she was wondering – was she about to be taken into some sort of back alley and "taken care of?"

Elizabeth sighed impatiently, flexing her hands out for a moment in front of her. "I *mean*, that there are certain matters that need to be considered, whenever someone wants to become seriously involved with a member of my family." Her mouth drew into a firm line. "The Thompson name is an old one, a well-respected one. It's powerful. We have money, political status, and a highly publicized social standing that can easily gain someone . . . notoriety."

She was giving her a considering look, one Sutton knew was not very flattering, and she narrowed her eyes as she cocked her head.

"I do consider myself lucky, with you," she continued. "Respect for your name in this country is nearly unparalleled. Your family has money and political stature." She nodded solidly, before pursing her lips and looking over Sutton in a once-over that made it feel as though Elizabeth had laser vision. "Luckily, that leads me to believe I don't have to worry that you would be using Charlotte on that front."

Indignation, hot and fast, slid through her. "I'm *not*."

Elizabeth continued as though she hadn't said anything. "You're a pretty woman, not unintelligent."

". . . thank you?" Was that a compliment? It felt far more like a slight and it left a bad taste in the back of her mouth.

"When it comes to Charlotte, it boils down to this – my granddaughter has staked everything to come out and be with you," her voice was low and commanding in an admirable way. That was, if Sutton wasn't well on her way to insult. "I implore you to consider this, young lady: Charlotte has a big future ahead of her. She needs a partner, a strong partner, not someone who will hold her back. You've got to decide sooner rather than later if you're willing to be that partner. Or, if this *is* some fleeting fancy of young love for you, then recognize it for what it is, and act accordingly."

She tapped her fingers on her desk as if to signal that was the final word, before leaning back in her chair and regarded Sutton with a challenging look.

For a few resounding moments they sat in silence and Sutton realized her mouth had literally fallen open in offense. Because Sutton could count on one hand how many times she'd felt this affronted and definitely never, ever, like this.

She'd never had her intentions questioned and her typically slow to boil temper burning hot through her veins.

"This is *not* a fleeting fancy of young love," she shot back, her voice low and angry, just a little out of breath. "I love Charlotte and I would never use her for anything." The energy blazing through her made her just restless enough to stand, tossing her hair over her shoulder. "I know exactly what Charlotte is risking by being with me, but she didn't come out just for me. She came out because *she's* strong and she doesn't need anyone to fight her battles for her."

After the words left her, Elizabeth slowly clasped her hands together in front of her as she tilted her head up to give Sutton another thoughtful look. "Hmm."

Only then did Sutton really realize where exactly she was and who she'd just spoken to like that.

She could feel her cheeks burn, the shock of it making her eyes widen as her hands fell to her sides. "I . . ." An apology was on the tip of her tongue but damn it, she didn't *want* to say it. Not after coming here just to be insulted. "I shouldn't have said . . . what I said . . . the way I said it," she finished, her stomach sinking. She just had to get out of there. "But I think you aren't giving Charlotte enough credit for her own choices and you certainly aren't giving me *any*."

Elizabeth continued to measure her up in silence – ugh, this was a disaster. It was going to be a disaster and she just knew that the mortification was going to set in at some point and she didn't want to be here when it did.

"I should, um, go. You have Chancellor Merkel on the phone."

"So I do, Miss Spencer," was all she got back in response, before Elizabeth reached for her phone as Sutton went to the door.

She thought for a moment that there was a hint of a *smile* on her face but she didn't stop and look. She quickly shut the door behind her and walked far too quickly out of the office.

First, her first serious job interview. Then her name and face and details of her relationship are being gossiped about all over the internet. Then Elizabeth Thompson herself summoning her to her office to imply that she is using Charlotte for – anything.

And then she yelled at her. At the *President*! Well, formerly, but still.

She might be sick to her stomach.

She barely even realized where exactly her feet had taken her in her power-walking, her hands buried in her coat pockets, until she looked up to realize . . . she'd unthinkingly walked several blocks. Several blocks, to Charlotte's uptown office.

Her assistant's desk was empty, giving Sutton a clear view right into the large glass window. She hadn't seen Charlotte in her office, yet – had only seen pictures of it all – and for just that moment, everything froze.

Charlotte stood facing out her window talking determinedly on her desk phone, leaving Sutton staring at her profile, and this maelstrom inside of her somewhat calmed.

She wore a pair of her fitted, tailored slacks, with a button-up top that had long sleeves folded up over her elbows. Sutton *knew* the cut of her jaw, just the way she tilted her head, that spoke of how resolute she was about whatever she was on the phone about. The way she smirked with her hand tapping smartly on her desk that the conversation was almost over.

It was awe-inspiring. Because Charlotte stood there in *her office*, that she'd won by making history already. By coming out and risking so much. And, yes it was for herself.

But it was also for *her*. For them. The implication was never lost on her, not in the last eight months since it'd happened, and it made her heart skip a beat.

That was her girlfriend. Her girlfriend, who was going to take over the world one day. In an amazing not-villainous way. But in the way that she was brilliant and well intentioned and was just so – lovely.

It was intimidating, sort of, because – she'd known it, peripherally. She'd always known Charlotte's ambition but she'd experienced it as something generally secondhand to herself.

But it wasn't secondhand anymore.

Charlotte's smirk turned into a sly grin as she hung up the phone and the sight of it nearly knocked her breath out of her lungs. That victorious, proud look that slid over her face was – she loved it.

Sutton knew the moment Charlotte saw her and a flash of confusion crossed her features. She tilted her head, a small confused smile tugging at her lips as she gestured for Sutton to come in.

She smiled back, a determined smile as her hands clenched tightly in her pockets for a moment before she took a deep breath. She entered the office, holding Charlotte's gaze.

"I'm strong," the words were out before she even thought about what she was going to say. But all she heard in her mind was what Elizabeth had said in her office.

Charlotte looked the most taken aback Sutton had ever seen. "I know you are?"

Which made Sutton want to roll her eyes at herself but she shook her head, her hair swinging over her shoulders as she pushed on. "I know it's not . . . I'm not the same as you are – perfect," she added on. "But I am here for you, as a partner. And I know our relationship has been somewhat atypical but I'm back here now and you're here, and we're together."

Charlotte regarded her for a long moment, a furrow between her eyebrows as she slowly tilted her head. "I take it this has something to do about this morning's gossip."

"Um. I was a little overwhelmed this morning," she hedged, admitting the somewhat truth.

Charlotte nodded slowly, taking in a deep breath. "I know it must have been a shock to see all that." A small frown pulled at her mouth and there was that slight look of uncertainty on her face, one that still threw Sutton a bit.

She'd seen it more in the last months than she had before Charlotte had come out. She'd seen it in times where Charlotte felt like she didn't know how to be a *girlfriend*, even though Sutton knew that was utterly ridiculous because she was the best girlfriend she could ever imagine.

"I want to be with you. And I can try to keep the media from you as much as I can," Charlotte spoke softly, regretfully. "But I'm afraid that this is only going to get more intense as the years go on."

Charlotte's eyes widened, as if she hadn't realized what she'd just said.

Sutton's stomach bottomed out only to fill with warmth, this mixture of love and affection as Charlotte cleared her throat. "Of course, I know this is still relatively new and years to come is a bit off to have to worry about –"

The upset that had propelled her to this point was completely gone, fading into the feeling in her chest that Charlotte so easily gave her. The tension she'd been carrying around since even before going to Elizabeth's office drained from her shoulders.

A smile spread over her face, unstoppable, as she took a step farther into the office. "I know I sounded," she broke off, biting her lip sheepishly, "A bit insane a moment ago. But I wanted to make the point that you don't need to keep me from anything." She came to a stop at the edge of Charlotte's desk, pulling her hands from her pockets and fiddling lightly with the ends of her sleeves. "I'm . . . I was uncomfortable this morning," she admitted. "Because I never really *thought* about it. But it's a part of being with you and I want that."

No matter what, she was sure of that.

She ran her eyes slowly over Charlotte, taking note of how her hair curled so naturally over her shoulder. Thinking about how she'd watched Charlotte quickly and efficiently yet perfectly style it this morning while she'd stood in her bathroom off of her bedroom, as Sutton had finished getting dressed.

It was so easy between them now and she couldn't deny that she reveled in it. In these simple domestic things that just happened so easily between them.

She brought her gaze back up to Charlotte's. "I want you for years to come."

A slow smile slid over Charlotte's face as she let out a low breath, "Well. Now that that's out of the way . . ." She reached out, tucking her fingertip into the waistband of Sutton's pants to tug her closer.

Her blood rushed a little warmer and she moved forward, close enough to feel her body warmth only inches from her own. Even as Charlotte wore her slight heels, Sutton was still just a bit taller, and she leaned down enough to brush her mouth over Charlotte's. She luxuriated for a few moments in the softness of her lips on her own.

It was light and brief, just enough to feel her, before they pulled back. Only inches away, her hand resting on the curve of Charlotte's hip as she whispered, "Hi."

She could feel Charlotte's slow grin without opening her eyes.

"Hi back, darling." Charlotte leaned up, brushing her lips softly against the side of Sutton's in the way that she had that was so close to being just a kiss on the cheek but wasn't. She didn't bother to hide the way it made her happily sigh, even as Charlotte pulled back.

"Want to join me for lunch before you go?" Charlotte asked, even though she was already pulling out the desk chair and gesturing for Sutton to sit in it.

She took the seat offered even as she said, "Well, I don't have anything to eat, but I'm happy to sit with you."

Charlotte gave her a dry look as she teased, "It just so happens that my girlfriend packed me a "lunch" that seems to hold enough food for the next three days, so I think we're okay on that front."

Sutton sniffed and tilted her head up. "Perhaps your girlfriend thinks you spend long hours at work and that you shouldn't forget to eat."

Brown eyes rolled at her, even as Charlotte couldn't contain that soft half-smile that Sutton knew was for her and her alone. She leaned against the desk in front of Sutton. "I suppose I can't argue with that."

"No, I suppose you can't." She reached out to interlock their fingers, just feeling their connection for a few seconds.

Elizabeth Thompson may have somewhat insulted her, but she supposed she did have a point. By being with Charlotte, Sutton had agreed to being in the public eye. And if there was a choice between having her life continue to be her own private life or having a life where she had to not be with Charlotte, there was no contest about what she would choose.

**

eliza harlow @elizathesapphic GOOD MORNING TWITTER LESBIANS *@thecharlottethompson showed up to prof @suttonspencer1's lit class to stare at her lovingly for a*N HOUR
11:43AM 02 OCT 22   2k Retweets 9k Likes

eliza harlow @elizathesapphic replying to @elizathesapphic
"wanted to see you in action" officially eavesdropped CALL 911 IM DYING 11:45AM 02 OCT 22

eliza harlow @elizathesapphic replying to @elizathesapphic
"see you at home darling" H OME THEY FUCKING LIVE TOGEHTER. WHEN DID THIS HAPPEN, SAPPHICS?
11:46AM 02 OCT 23

taylor~BLM~ @spencesonRISE replying to @elizathesapphic who cares when it happened! We love to see it!!! 11:47AM 02 OCT 22

Kenzie @misskenzington *replying to @elizathesapphic How tf long are we waiting before they take over the world?!* 11:47AM 02 OCT 22

Part 3

Charlotte, overall, enjoyed spending the holidays with the Spencer family.

There were some negatives: the weather, for one. Despite having been with Sutton for over three years now and spending each of those holiday seasons with the Spencers – if she was counting their unofficial beginning as the start of their relationship, which they did – Charlotte was used to spending the holidays in the south.

But she remedied that by spending the majority of her time indoors and finding it a perfect excuse to curl up close to Sutton whenever possible. Including slipping her hands under her girlfriend's sweater when they were cold, as well as falling impossibly more for Sutton when she shivered and would laughingly protest, but would always stand still to be Charlotte's personal heater.

This being her third Christmas spent with the Spencer family, she knew what to expect and she genuinely *liked* it.

She liked them, individually, as people. She enjoyed seeing them interact as a family, and she loved seeing the bright, happy way Sutton smiled with them. At home, she'd seen and heard Sutton call and video chat with all of her family members more times than she could count, but it was different in person.

And she found being welcomed into their traditions was far smoother and more natural than she'd expected it would be.

The first year they'd been together, when Sutton had been somewhat shy as she asked Charlotte – all rambling – if she would want to join her in Boston for the holidays, Charlotte had almost said no; she'd only been stopped because she already *knew* how disappointed Sutton would have been, and subsequently would have tried to hide.

But the fact of the matter was that, even at that point, after having been with Sutton for almost a year and having known her for longer than that, the idea of staying with her family was honestly nerve-wracking. But if she wanted to be with Sutton, the family aspect came with that.

And she'd been pleasantly surprised. It hadn't been uncomfortable, not really, not as she made easy conversation with Oliver, given their similar professions, and Alex, given how she'd gotten to know her back home in the months prior.

She enjoyed decorating the tree with them, while the Spencer siblings argued and laughed and told loud stories about one another. She enjoyed their family viewing of classic movies on Christmas Eve. She enjoyed their tradition of Christmas morning cinnamon buns before opening gifts.

It wasn't as though she hadn't enjoyed the holiday growing up. But her own family had never been the same as Sutton's was.

William had been years older than both she and Caleb, and their parents had always been busy, as had her grandmother. Holidays growing up hadn't been about quality time, which had been just fine for her at the time. She hadn't really known how much fun quality time like this could have been, until now.

She liked all of these things far, far more than she'd ever thought she would. And she was more comfortable partaking in them than she could have possibly imagined by now.

This year, she'd been looking forward to being here even more than she had in previous years. Because she'd taken a flight in from D.C., where she'd been at a conference for the last two weeks. The conference had been challenging and productive, but extremely busy and had given her some new prospects to think over. But as much as she hated to admit it, a few days of relaxing here would do her well.

It just wasn't as easy for her to sleep at night at conferences without Sutton there. Especially not now, after Sutton had moved in with her last year. Now that she was so used to having her in bed every night, sleeping alone felt almost unnatural.

But she couldn't let herself revel in that – the fact that after almost three weeks of craving her girlfriend, she got to have her tonight – not even as she was standing in Sutton's old bedroom.

"Where is it," she murmured under her breath, letting out a frustrated sigh, her hands flexing on her hips as she surveyed the bed. She'd taken *everything* out of her suitcases.

They were laying empty on the floor next to her, and everything that could have possibly been inside of them in any pocket was emptied and organized in front of her, but there was something missing.

A very specific gift.

Most of the holiday gifts to the Spencer family were from both herself and Sutton. Of course, Sutton was the driving force behind the ideas, but Charlotte added her own add-ons or accents last year, too, because – well, the Spencer's were now not only just her-girlfriends-family, but were people she had gotten to know herself and cared about.

But she knew that Sutton had packed and brought most of their joint gifts for her family when she'd arrived a week ago.

The only gifts she'd intended to pack herself were the ones she'd bought for Sutton… and the one she'd gotten for Katherine.

She knew, of course, that Sutton had gotten her mother a gift. One that she would love, because Sutton always found gifts for everyone that they loved, let alone the fact that Kate and Charlotte had one specific thing in common, and it was an adoration in almost anything Sutton did.

But *her* gift for Katherine had to be different. She couldn't simply give the joint gift with Sutton, like they did for everyone else.

Charlotte narrowed her eyes, quickly tying her hair up to keep it from irritatingly falling into her eyes, as she bent down to rifle through everything yet again.

"There's no way I could have forgotten it," she muttered, before she tilted her head.

Could she have forgotten it? It was so incredibly unlike her, but she had been somewhat in a rush to pack, and had to pack for both her business trip and then her holiday trip. All the while, Sutton had been doing some sort of advanced power yoga on the other side of their bedroom, and she'd been… easily distracted.

"There's no way you could have forgotten what?" Sutton's voice came from behind her, moments before her arms wrapped around Charlotte's waist, as she placed her chin on Charlotte's shoulder to look at all of the items spread out before them. "You unpacked quickly. I was only downstairs helping with dinner for a few minutes!"

It gave her just a momentary relaxation, melting back into Sutton and breathing her in, loving the feeling of Sutton's body pressed against her back, and the effortless way she supported her. God, but she always missed her so incredibly much during trips to the capital.

She only allowed herself another deep breath there, though, before she sighed, and her eyebrows furrowed as she surveyed everything in front of her again. "The gift I got your mother," she answered.

Her hands came to cover Sutton's, stroking her fingertips over her knuckles, before she huffed out a breath in agitation. "But it's not *here*," her mounting exasperation was back, as she gestured to everything she'd unpacked, "How am I supposed to win over your mother like this? I spent *months* tracking that first edition poetry book down and it's not here!"

There was a choked laugh in her ear. "Win over my mother?"

She groaned, softly, the irritation with herself for most certainly not having the gift packed welling up inside. "Yes, because she doesn't like me," she stated, matter-of-factly.

Sutton's mother was the only other downside of holidays with the Spencer's. Objectively, she was lovely. Watching her with Sutton actually *warmed* Charlotte inside in such an odd way. She was a smart woman, a talented woman, and Charlotte respected her. But it was Katherine with her polite and just-warm-enough-to-not-be-cold smiles directed right toward her that was the worst part of the holiday.

It wasn't as though she seemed to hate her, Charlotte knew that… but she also knew that she was granted graciousness because of her relationship with Sutton. She'd managed to win over, in some way, every other member of the Spencer family – even Jack!

Jack Spencer, who notoriously disliked most other politicians, was on a friendly weekly email basis with her! She regularly texted with Oliver and even Alex, and had been in some group chats with the other Spencer siblings. And yet, it was Katherine who was the hold out, after three years.

A disbelieving scoff left Sutton's mouth, big blue eyes staring down at her in surprise as Sutton adjusted enough to the side so she could remain standing behind Charlotte but still be able to look her in the eye. "She does not dislike you!"

Charlotte let out a deep breath, turning enough to arch her eyebrow at Sutton. Just giving her the *look*, because there was no way to deny it.

Not when their interactions were always the same as they'd been a couple of hours earlier.

Sutton had picked her up from the airport, brought her back to the Spencer home. And when they'd walked into the house through the kitchen, Katherine had looked up with a bright, sincere smile to her daughter. And then when her gaze had shifted to Charlotte, the spark dimmed notably. The corners of her mouth notched downward, chilling her smile just a bit. She'd tilted her head, the sheer warmth of her tone when she'd greeted Sutton replaced with what Charlotte could only describe as an impersonally genial tone, *"Charlotte, I'm glad you made it in time for the holidays. It's nice to see you."*

And it never seemed to matter what she did or said. She'd imported Katherine's favorite kind of wine from Europe for a birthday gift. When Katherine had complimented her on the finely knit scarf she'd purchased from a designer in Italy that she'd worn on her first Christmas, she'd then contacted the designer and had another made, and sent it to Katherine. She'd had a delicate custom-made blown glass family tree of the Spencer family that she *knew* Katherine loved, as it was displayed over the mantle in the den, last Christmas, but still.

Polite warmth.

Her mouth just in a line as she lifted her eyebrow at Sutton, daring her to disagree again. She knew her girlfriend wouldn't, just by the way she felt her shuffle behind her for a moment, even before her eyes dropped to look at the ground and she bit her lip.

"She doesn't *dis*like you…" Sutton hedged, her cheeks flushing, "She just – doesn't know you all that well." Charlotte didn't point out that Katherine never seemed all too interested in spending more time with her. "Besides," Sutton spoke softly, her voice a bit more playful but still honest, "It isn't as though your grandmother likes me, either, and I see her *all* of the time."

Which was – well, only sort of true, and honeyed brown eyes narrowed. "It's different."

Sutton's mouth fell open in offense, as she flexed her hands on Charlotte's hips. "It is not!"

"It *is*," she explained, "My grandmother doesn't like anyone; when it comes to people romantically involved in her grandchildren's lives, she likes you the most. Her liking you the most just also entails her being critical. She *never* willingly invites Dean to lunch," she reminded her, and it was all the honest truth.

Clearly the situations were miles different.

She knew that Sutton didn't necessarily see it, but Charlotte knew that her grandmother had started to be won over by Sutton bit by bit after the first year.

After Sutton had proven time and time again that she wasn't backing down, after she'd grown more poised in the face of the media, after she'd weathered a few lunches with Elizabeth and hadn't wilted like the wallflower her grandmother expected her to be.

There was this warm feeling inside of her at that, deep in the pit of her stomach. It was pride in Sutton, partially. Because God only knew that it took someone special to handle her grandmother, and she'd known how special Sutton was from the very beginning, but it didn't make the reminders of it any less wondrous.

But it was that... that despite Charlotte's long hours and oftentimes borderline obsession with work, her critically demanding grandmother, and the fact that everything was so public, Sutton never wavered. She was always solidly by Charlotte's side, and she was so utterly lovely that –

Charlotte wanted to give her everything back, in spades. Sutton had, for all intents and purposes, won over her grandmother, which made Charlotte feel so incredibly happy.

And she wanted to win over Katherine, too, if for no other reason than for Sutton to know that her mother, whose guidance, support, and approval meant the world to her, approved of Charlotte, too.

There was another reason, of course, being that Charlotte could not *stand* the fact that her girlfriend's mother disliked her. She didn't mind being disliked by certain people. Political rivals, those who foundationally opposed what she stood for and what she was fighting for – they could go to all hell. Sometimes she even reveled in their disdain.

But when it came to other people, there was the drive in her that she couldn't get rid of to win them over. Which was typically just fine, because *typically* Charlotte didn't have trouble winning anyone over!

Was it so wrong to want the woman she was in love with's mother to like her?

The thought made her groan, dropping her head back and landing on Sutton's shoulder, the stress and frustration she only allowed herself to openly feel with Sutton on display. "I just don't understand it."

Her voice held an exasperation edge that she didn't even like to hear from herself, before she pushed forward to spin and face her girlfriend.

Sutton's face was a vision of sympathy, as she ran her hand up Charlotte's spine. "What?"

"Why doesn't she like me?" She hated that those words even came out of her mouth, but she couldn't help it. "Like, I understand her loving Jane. She's known her for almost ten years now and is the mother of her grandchild. But what about Chris?"

She knew Sutton was trying to hold back a laugh and she was barely doing a decent job. "What about Chris?"

"He lives in Manhattan, too! She sees me just as often – if not more – than she sees him. He and Alex only *just* became official, after dating for years. And yet she loves him!" The whine in her voice was apparent and if she was talking to literally anyone else in the world it would have shamed her.

Sutton gave her a gentle smile. "Um. Well, I mean, Chris really doesn't have anyone, you know? He's sort of like this little lamb that my mom feels she needs to take care of."

Charlotte considered it, and begrudged, "Fine. I don't want to be a little lamb," she grumbled, thinking she would take polite coolness above that. But still. She narrowed her eyes, knowing unequivocally that she had her next point in the bag, "Isla."

The chuckle that broke from Sutton's lips before she could stop it only spurred her on.

"She likes Isla! Isla, who swears more than anyone else I've ever heard and gave Ethan a *knife* last year for Christmas?" She challenged, tossing her hands in the air. "I mean, come on!"

Sutton was full-out laughing now, the laughter making her cheeks flush, her eyes sparkling, and it made Charlotte want to smile just watching her, even as much as she held onto her pout. "It's not funny."

Sutton managed to quell her laughter, but was still smiling widely at her, as she reached out to pull Charlotte even closer. "I love you."

She moved against Sutton, pressing against her, looping her arms around Sutton's neck. "I love you, too, which is why this isn't funny."

But a small smile tugged at her lips as Sutton continued to smile, ducking down to press their mouths together. Slowly, lightly at first, then a bit more insistent.

It wasn't funny, but… it could not be funny while she lost herself in Sutton.

It was a couple of hours, a luxuriously languid heated making out with Sutton, and a dinner with all of the Spencer family full of those politely warm smiles from Katherine while seeing how she gave everyone else at the table the real thing, that found them cuddled up in the den, on the couch in front of the fireplace, which happened to be Charlotte's favorite place in the house.

Despite having forgotten her gift for Katherine, Charlotte was – for now, though she knew her discontent about the situation would return come morning – too content to care. She was comfortable and relaxed and so warm, sitting on one of these cushy couches, wrapped up in one of the blankets from Sutton's bed that smelled so perfectly like her. As Sutton's head was pillowed in her lap, and she lightly stroked her fingers through her hair.

The holidays, she'd learned with Sutton, for any of the other stressful moments, were good for this. For these soft, quiet times.

"Tell me more about your conference," Sutton broke off from humming quietly along with the holiday music playing from her phone, her voice slow and lazy, the way it always got when she was cuddled and comfortable past eleven at night.

Charlotte shifted slightly, careful not to dislodge Sutton from where she rested against her, before blowing out a quiet, considering sigh. "I viscerally felt the way my grandmother has often described these conferences – that they go on forever when, if everyone was focused, we could have been finished in half the time." Sutton hummed in half agreement and half amusement at Charlotte's eyeroll, even if she couldn't see it. "But, it was all right."

She felt Sutton shake her head just a bit. "You said there was something you wanted to talk about from it? With me," she clarified, and her voice was dipping into the low, slow rasp she got when she was sleepy.

It was actually one of Charlotte's favorite sounds, the way Sutton's voice curled over the words as they formed in her mind, and she wrestled against falling asleep.

"Mm," she thought for a moment, slipping her hand under the neck of Sutton's sweater, running her nails lightly over her shoulder blades. "The first thing is that I finally got some backing for the youth shelter proposal I've been trying to push through."

She paused for a moment, weighing the thoughts that had been constantly in the back of her mind since she'd heard them a few days ago, before she murmured, "The second is that I found out that Mathew Rowan isn't running for re-election as Governor because of his health; he's announcing it in less than a month."

She drew her hand up, massaging over the back of Sutton's neck, enjoying the feeling of her warmth so close. "Which means there will be a serious election next year."

"And I know it's a few years sooner than I planned to run for anything again, but I can't help this feeling that – I want it. It worked before, after all, to get into the House. Running a bit earlier than I had planned, and look at us now." She smiled before she took in a deep breath and held it, thinking over all of the possibilities and outcomes and options.

"So, I think I want to do it. I think I'm ready for the race." At the very least, more experience under her belt could only be a good thing.

Her eyebrows drew together, though, the negatives of a campaign coming to mind. "But we need to talk, first. Obviously, a campaign is – trying. The hours and the work and the publicity is going to be even more of a circus than it was the last time." And even though the dust had certainly settled in the past couple of years, this would just kick it all up again.

Brown eyes drifted down to watch her own hand as she toyed with the hair on the nape of Sutton's neck. "I need to consider your time constraints, with the courses you're taking on. And if you're ready, yet, for a big election, together," she caught herself just voicing her thoughts as they came to mind, rambling almost exactly like Sutton. "We have some time to think about it and talk it over, of course. I want you to take your time with this. Well, as much time as we have to decide, anyway. If right now isn't good for you, then we'll wait until the next election. Okay, darling?"

She stroked her fingers slowly through Sutton's hair as she looked down after a few beats of silence went by.

And found bright blue eyes closed, her breathing coming softly, with her fingers curled lightly into the blanket just under Charlotte's thigh.

The firelight moved gently over Sutton's features, and she shook her head slightly, a smile tugging at her lips as she gently traced her fingertips over Sutton's forehead, then ever so lightly down her nose, "So beautiful," she whispered to herself, hearing her own wistfulness, before she settled back into the couch, her eyes growing heavy with the warmth around her and Sutton against her.

She wasn't surprised to be alone when she woke up the next morning. They'd moved from the den to Sutton's room after she herself had dozed off for a few minutes – and by the time they'd gone into Sutton's old room, they'd both woken up enough to make up for the two weeks in which they hadn't been together.

And despite the fact that they'd been tangled up in one another until nearly three in the morning, it was typical for Sutton to be awake before eight the next morning. Especially on holidays, when her entire family full of morning people were also already awake.

It was also typical for Sutton to tiptoe around and let Charlotte sleep for as long as she possibly could, even when Charlotte wouldn't have minded getting up.

Still, it was just after nine and she knew, as it was the day before Christmas Eve, that the Spencers and their significant others would be engaged in annual holiday snowball warfare. She, having never been one who enjoyed even gym class let alone… that, but especially as someone who would rather not be out in the cold for any extended amount of time, gave Sutton her ideas for strategizing a win for her team, and would remain indoors, abstaining from the fight at hand.

She wrapped the throw blanket that she knew Sutton had tucked around her before she'd gotten up over her shoulders, rubbing at her still slightly bleary eyes as she made her way down into the kitchen.

After some coffee and checking her work email, she figured she would probably align her schedule in time for Sutton to come in from snowball warfare and they could shower together.

And she nearly groaned when, as she walked through the doorway into the kitchen, she realized she was not as alone as she'd thought.

She'd only pulled her hair up into a tangled, curling bun without even brushing it first, wearing Sutton's sweatpants that she frequently stole at home and had to curl at the waist so that they didn't drag on the floor, and was looking generally as un-put-together as anyone who was not her girlfriend ever saw her.

And of course, this would be the only morning she'd ever spent in the Spencer home where Katherine was both home after eight in the morning and wasn't upstairs in her writing office.

It wasn't as though Charlotte *dressed up* on typical days spent at Sutton's family's home. But unless it was a rare morning when everyone else was already up and about and busy, she generally always showered and dressed before she saw anyone who wasn't Sutton. No matter who you were with, she knew, the appearance you gave off mattered.

She'd gleaned from her own powers of observation that Katherine always left the house bright and early to run any errands she had to do, or took the time to get to work. And there were times where she'd set up shop at the breakfast nook in the kitchen, but those times had always, in the past, been in the evening. And those were times that she'd often welcome interruptions or input from her family. Charlotte's input on her writing had never been something she'd asked for.

As it was, Charlotte took a breath and stood up straight; she certainly wouldn't *hide* from Katherine, as she didn't hide from anyone. And it was too late to turn without looking odd.

"Good morning, Charlotte," Katherine's expected greeting came. Only… Charlotte gave her a small smile, receiving one in return – and her mind may have been playing tricks on her, because it seemed a modicum warmer than the one she typically got?

"Good morning," she echoed curiously, padding over to the coffee maker. When Katherine didn't say anything, Charlotte bit back a sigh; she supposed she had been reading into it. "I'll be quick, I don't want to disturb you."

She poured her coffee into a mug, only pausing slightly when she saw from the window that she had been right, and it was snowball warfare time. The Spencers were spread out through the visible yard, and their home bases were already built and fortified – and she saw that Sutton's had a trench dug off to the side of hers, which had been Charlotte's suggestion to hide in – and it made her smile indulgently.

It was then that Katherine cleared her throat. "Actually, I've been hoping to catch a moment with you, if you wouldn't mind having a seat."

Shock raced through her, because never once in three years had Katherine actually seemed to want to spend much time with her. She wasn't sure whether or not to feel excitement or trepidation, and instead remained on the fence, as she cradled her mug and moved to join her. "Of course. Is there something on your mind?"

She vaguely wondered if somehow Katherine knew she'd left her Christmas present at home. Truly, she had no idea what she could want to talk about, and she wracked her brain. Three years, three Christmases, dozens of trips Kate had taken to Manhattan, sporadic times Charlotte had joined Sutton on smaller trips to Boston… and not once had she expressed interest in having genuine conversation with Charlotte that was beyond perfunctory.

"Still not one for the cold?" Katherine asked, a small conspiratorial grin that had never been directed at her was on her mouth, as she gestured at the blanket pulled around Charlotte.

And she found herself tugging it closer, a surprised grin mirroring back. "Yes, I'm sorry to say, I doubt I'll ever find myself wanting to have a snowball fight."

"There's nothing wrong with that. I've gotten used to the weather, but I do prefer the indoors during these winter months, especially. Trust that I certainly did not play many snowball fights with the children."

Charlotte cautioned a smile, despite the fact that she'd heard many stories of Katherine putting up with the cold in order to walk through the trails with her children and even play with them in the snow. "I'm sure I've heard some tales to the contrary. Sutton's told me many about what adventures you would think up for them."

Her voice was measured, casual, even as her mind still wondering what this was about.

Before Katherine sighed and the smile on her face dropped a bit as she tapped her fingers against her own mug of what Charlotte was sure was tea. "I love all of my children more than life itself."

It was far from what Charlotte had been expecting her to say and she blinked for a moment, getting into the right headspace.

"Yes," she nodded. "I think anyone who has ever seen you with them could see that."

It brought a ghost of a smile back to Katherine's face, as she tilted her head as if to say *touché*. "I would do anything for all of them. Maybe because my own mother died so young, I've never taken my chance to be a *mom* for granted. To know them all as individual people. Which also means that I know very well what I truly believe they need in a partner," she paused, looking up across the kitchen for a moment as if searching for words.

"Alex, for instance. Has always needed to march to the beat to her own drummer. To push harder, be stronger, tougher than anyone who challenged her. And for her to truly thrive, she would need to find someone who understood that, who would challenge her but understand that she needs independence. Chris so clearly knows that. I've never doubted it for a second," she turned then, eyes no longer searching for the words. "And Sutton... my Sutton, has always been a romantic. Big hearted, and willing to strike out in search for her own purpose. Which means she's always opened her heart entirely to those she's fallen for. She can devote herself so much to someone that I'm worried she'd forget herself, with the wrong partner." Those blue eyes landed on her, as if appraising her on the spot. "And she's never fallen for anyone the way she has for you."

Ah.

Charlotte took the words in, feeling pinned down by them, by the utter knowing conviction in her tone, and she narrowed her eyes in defense. "Sutton does have the biggest heart." She acknowledged, because it was so *true*, and she got to revel in it every day. "And I know I don't have the same quality. But I do love her."

It was a promise she made with conviction, because it was true. She wouldn't dare say she possessed the same kind of open heart that Sutton did, but she knew that no one had ever made hers full in the way that Sutton had.

And perhaps, then, if her devotion to Sutton was what had kept Katherine from accepting her, then maybe they could resolve this once and for all.

But Kate shook her head. "While I've been reserved about you, I know you love my daughter. I'm not blind."

She could feel the tension in her shoulders and for once, allowed the frustrated breath to fall from her mouth, rather than the practiced politeness and acceptance she always mirrored back. "Then why? *Why* are you so reserved about me, if you can see how much I love her?"

It was so confusing to her, as to why that of all things made Katherine genuinely smile. "I think you are exceptionally intelligent, Charlotte. Smarter at reading people than anyone I've ever met, and that says quite a bit about you."

She paused to take a sip of her tea, her words not seeming positive or negative, just *honest*. And Charlotte couldn't quite figure out where she was going with it.

"But I also think that means you know exactly what people want to hear. You know exactly how to charm and enchant and give people what they want. Or, how to make people think you're giving them what they want; which is a tremendous skill, one I even can admire," she acknowledged, but now Charlotte was finally hearing what she'd been looking for – a hint at the disapproval to come. "And it's exactly what I don't trust about you."

The vocalized disapproval she'd been waiting on pins and needles to receive for years.

And the worst part is that she couldn't even deny it, because it was something Charlotte prided herself on. Something necessary for her chosen life.

She took a sip of her coffee, maintaining eye contact with Katherine as she did so. Because she wanted her approval, but she wasn't sorry for who she was.

"You've known me for only a few years," she continued, "And you've figured out exactly what holiday and birthday gifts to get me – something some members of my own family can struggle with. But you had a read on me despite my keeping a distance. I think you're a fantastic politician, who knows just how to play in a world of pretense. Related to that, frankly, I've been very concerned that your life is too public, too harsh, and that *you* are just a bit too much – too ambitious and too focused – to juggle who you are, with who Sutton deserves to be with."

There it was. What Charlotte had been trying to figure out for years, laid out in front of her. And it actually hurt to hear, more than she'd expected. She took it in, looking down at her coffee for a moment as she bit at her cheek, because it felt like such a blow.

Perhaps because that was the thing she worried about the most when it came to her ability to be a good girlfriend to Sutton. But despite having those insecurities, she *knew* how much she valued Sutton's happiness, her comfort.

"I suppose my gifts, and the fact that I always maintain my appearance to be put together hasn't been in my favor," she began, but – was there really anything she could say to dispel those particular thoughts?

She could make all kinds of promises, about exactly how much she not only loved Sutton but valued her, respected her choices and needs. But, wasn't that the issue? How did she get Katherine to trust her words when she already expected them to be disingenuous?

"You're correct about that," Kate allowed, tilting her head toward her, before she regarded Charlotte carefully. "But what is in your favor, is that I heard you talk to my daughter last night, about the future. And please excuse me because I didn't intend to eavesdrop, but I was checking that the doors were all locked last night and you were in the den with the door ajar."

It was surprising to feel embarrassment, because she rarely ever did. But she did at that moment, refusing to let herself squirm, even as she cleared her throat. "Oh."

Katherine's hand reached out to cover hers, though, stilling even the urge to squirm. "And I know now that I've misjudged you." She squeezed, causing Charlotte to look at her. "I've always worried about Sutton being so far from home. I feel a bit better knowing that she has someone like you in her corner."

"She does," the words came out softer than she intended, but it was impossible to feel any semblance of embarrassment this time.

Because the smile on Katherine's face was that of actual *warmth*, and a bit of vulnerability was worth this victory.

***

21.4k Votes | Charlotte Thompson and Sutton Spencer
17.9k Comments   Posted by Monica_Mc 3 Years Ago

ewdavid *262 votes | Okay, but they are definitely engaged?? Did anyone else notice their pictures from the concert last night? There are rings, people!*

Kelsi *25 votes | I mean. Just because they're wearing rings doesn't mean anything, though. Charlotte just lost her election for governor a month ago... seems like weird timing. Also am I the only one who remembers them talking about how they aren't rushing into anything and like to take their relationship slowly?*

lilaceyes *341 votes | I wouldn't say getting married after four years is rushing into anything LOL*

QueenSansa *975 votes | They finally posted on their IGs! It's official! We're getting a fall Spenceson wedding yall!*

3/09/24

Part 4

Sutton had imagined planning a wedding for a long time. She'd planned her own several times over throughout her youth and she'd never really thought of herself as being very fanciful. In fact, she actually believed many of her wedding details from her teenage years were meticulously planned, even now, at thirty.

But what she hadn't considered, really, in those youthful plans, was the fact that she would be marrying a woman.

More than that, she never exactly figured she would be getting married to a woman who was likely to become a senator in less than a year, who had a former president as a grandmother, or who had Charlotte's parents.

Though she'd been with Charlotte for almost six years, she'd only met Alison and Mitchell Thompson about nine or ten times. It was a far cry from the now familiar relationship she had with Elizabeth – not that she would necessarily call Elizabeth fond of her, exactly, as she was a very hard woman to please. But they saw one another very regularly, occasionally without Charlotte. It was an even bigger difference from the relationship Charlotte had with *her* family.

To say the relationship her soon-to-be wife had with her parents confused Sutton would be the biggest understatement. Charlotte spent weeks without getting a call or text from them and didn't think anything of it. They didn't think anything of not spending holidays together.

Even last year, when she'd tentatively proposed they spend some of the holiday season with the Thompson's rather than the entire week with her own family, Charlotte had given her the most puzzled look.

"What do you mean? We always go to your parents' house for the holidays."

Sutton had gesticulated wildly because, "*Exactly*. We're engaged now and I've never spent more than a meal with either of your parents. Don't you think that's…" She'd bit her lip, because she didn't want to insult Charlotte or her parents, even though she could *never* understand their dynamic. "Weird?"

Her fiancée had taken a few beats with a contemplative frown, doing what Sutton knew she always did – give every angle of a situation a full thought breakdown. Before she answered slowly, "I suppose it is. But it's not…" A small sigh escaped her, as she pushed her hand through her hair. "I know that my relationship with them isn't the most normal. And now that I know what it's like to have what your family has, I think about it. But it is who they are and that's okay. Just very hands-off most of the time."

There were a thousand questions Sutton had, most of them regarding the concern she had for Charlotte and how their distance affected her. If it did.

Charlotte's sly but sweet grin flashed over her face then, as she'd grabbed Sutton's hips and pulled her close. She let out a yelp, concerns fleeing as she found herself squarely on her lap.

"It's a sweet thought, darling. But my parents are going to France for the holidays with some friends, anyway."

So, really, it came as an utter shock to her that Alison became so involved in the wedding planning. Sutton had been shocked when the woman – a near spitting image of Charlotte, if she added on twenty-five years and was instead a blonde – came strutting into their home months ago, wanting to go over every detail that had already been planned.

She hadn't factored in the fact that Alison and Mitchell had high-society guests and expectations. She also hadn't factored in Elizabeth's own standards. What was always bound to be a rather large and lavish affair, given both her family and Charlotte herself, had soon turned into the biggest event of the year.

It wasn't as though she'd thought her significant other would have *no* input in the wedding… but she'd really thought she and her mother would have the majority of the say in the matter. It wasn't that she was unhappy with the decisions that had been made or that she didn't have a final say in most matters – especially because Charlotte typically seconded whatever she wanted.

It was just… a lot.

She didn't want to complain. Not when Charlotte was already so busy with preparing her senate campaign and was always jumping into wedding planning whenever she had a free second.

Not when she was getting married to the love of her life, regardless of the details.

There were debates about where it should be held – Manhattan, Boston, or Virginia – that lasted for what seemed like decades, which was *after* a destination had been ruled out. Both she and Charlotte had quickly put their foot down on that.

A Virginia wedding had won out in the end. Married in the luxurious rose gardens in the Thompson mansion courtyard, especially as the Thompson family home was also large enough to house the entire wedding party and the grounds could easily serve as a beautiful, convenient reception.

Sutton heaved out a deep sigh as she remained on the bed in Charlotte's childhood room. More like suite, that had either been redone since Charlotte had lived here or, more likely, it had always looked like this. Too elegant for a child to have properly lived in it.

Regan echoed her sigh from where she lay, flung next to Sutton on the bed. She'd followed her back to the room over an hour ago, after wrapping everything up for the night.

"Damn. Growing up, I always thought you were rich. After that rehearsal dinner with the Thompson horde…" She broke off on a low whistle.

A laugh worked its way out of her throat as she nodded. "Tell me about it."

The dinner had been, like much of the plans for the wedding tomorrow, extravagant. More people than she would have possibly imagined would be at the rehearsal dinner – there were clearly some additions to the list when she and Charlotte weren't looking.

Which – was fine. It was fine. Not exactly what she'd thought, but it was okay.

They sat side-by-side in silence for a few moments, looking around her bride-to-be's room, before both of their gazes landed on Sutton's wedding dress. It was hanging pristinely in the garment bag in front of the bay window. The sweetheart top with intricate beading, before it cinched at the waist to flow down to the floor… it had been something there'd been no debate over. Sutton had known it as soon as she'd put it on, as had everyone else in the room with her.

Regan's warm hand landed on hers. "Festivities start tomorrow at three in the afternoon. That gives us sixteen hours to abscond into the night. One last chance to duck out of here and just be Sutton and Regan again. What do you say?"

She couldn't help but laugh. "I say Emma might have a problem with that."

Regan giggled. "Yeah. But Segan would live forever."

"Segan?"

"Our couple name, duh."

Blue eyes rolled as she pushed her shoulder into Regan's. "How dumb of me."

A beat went by before she felt Regan turn her head to look at her. "It's really happening, then. You're getting *married*. To Stunning Charlotte Thompson."

Sutton turned her head to look at Regan too, mirroring her pose as both of them leaned their heads back onto the headboard. "It's really happening." The warmth in her stomach that moved up to fill her chest was what made the smile on her face appear and refuse to leave even as she rolled her eyes. "Even with all of the extra… pomp and circumstance."

Regan ignored her – interesting, given that her best friend had many choice comments about how their original wedding plans had all been blown out of proportion. "So, when's the wife due back to your room?"

Sutton checked her watch. It was after eleven now and Charlotte had ducked after the rehearsal dinner with a quick kiss, almost two hours ago. "Any minute now, I guess. She had to wrap up some last minute stuff." She knew how much finagling Charlotte had done to take off the next two weeks for a proper honeymoon.

Sutton hadn't minded having to postpone it; she understood that was what she was signing up for with Charlotte. But her fiancée had insisted.

"I think we have enough time." Regan vaguely stated before she hopped off the bed and quickly ran to where her dress was hung up.

"Time for what?" She pushed herself up, confused, as her best friend grabbed the dress and held it out to her.

"Time for you to give me a final fashion show." Regan wiggled her eyebrows exaggeratedly, before she walked the dress over to Sutton. "Come on. I want to see you in it."

Sutton scoffed. "You're going to see me in it tomorrow, lunatic. I'm not putting it on tonight."

Regan aimed her with a *look*. "You're going to tell me, Sutton Spencer, that you haven't tried this dress on religiously? Because if my best friend hasn't been butterflies-in-the-stomach-every-night level excited before her wedding… I *am* going to abscond with you in the night so you don't make a mistake."

Sutton *tried* to glare. She really did. But the corners of her lips pulled up in a reluctant smile. "*Fine*. Fine. I may have tried it on a few times since I got it from the seamstress."

Regan's triumph was palpable. She started pulling down the zipper of the garment bag, humming an over-the-top wedding march.

Before Sutton couldn't contain herself anymore and, "Okay! But only for a few minutes. Charlotte hasn't seen my dress yet and I don't want her walking in."

Twenty minutes later, she'd changed and was staring at herself in the full-length mirror, running her hands down the bodice. Regan was standing next to her, giving them a nice picture with her in her wedding dress and her best friend in the dress she'd worn to the rehearsal dinner.

Her friends' eyes were wide and serious. "I know I've seen you in it before, but... Jesus Christ, Sutton."

She found herself with an armful of Regan, her arms banded around her waist tightly. "You're getting *married*."

"Yeah," she breathed back, hugging her friend just as hard. "Tomorrow."

As Regan pulled back, her eyes were watery, even with her mischievous glint. "And I hope you know that I'm always going to hold it over you two that it was my doing. It will be the last thing I say on my deathbed."

"As if you ever let us forget it." Sutton slid her hands to her friends forearms, squeezing.

She froze at the knock on the door. Before she hopped as best she could in her floor-length gown as it opened, trying to figure out a way to get behind the changing screen. Alarm shooting through her, she hissed at Regan, "Charlotte can't see me yet!"

As the door swung open, though, it revealed Emma. She arched an eyebrow at the two of them as Regan beamed at her. And Sutton's entire body relaxed. It was one of their only surprise agreements – for neither of them to know what the other's dress would look like before the day.

"Do I have perfect timing or what?" Regan proclaimed.

"We're all ready." Was all Emma said before she grinned softly and shook her head slightly at Regan. A fondness she wanted to pretend was exasperation after all these years. She turned to look at Sutton and a different smile slid over her face. "You look amazing."

"Thanks. But what are you ready for?" Suspicion curled low in her stomach as she crossed her arms to look at Regan. "I told you – no more bachelorette party extravaganzas. I mean it."

Regan took her role as Maid of Honor very seriously. And had proven it by not having one big bachelorette party. But instead there had been – so far – four "extravaganzas" as Regan labeled them.

Her best friend immediately looked affronted, then defensive. "Okay, hear me out!" She rushed to continue before Sutton could argue. "We had the Regan and Sutton night. Then us three. Then with us and Alex and Alia. *Then* the party back in Boston with Isla and Jane. But we haven't had anything where the entire bachelorette party has been able to all gather in one place. Tonight is the only night! And it'll be quick. We're all just going to have some champagne and tell some stories about how much we love your sunshine face."

Which, all right, Regan had a point. Because of everyone's schedules and locations, they *hadn't* been able to all have a time where they were all together.

She pursed her lips. "Tomorrow is going to be so long and I want to have some time here with Charlotte before we go to bed." But both of them knew her resolve was nonexistent. Still, though, this was Regan. "I mean it."

Regan turned to look at Emma, who was watching them both with her hands on her hips. "Can you vouch for me here, babe?"

Emma arched a teasing eyebrow before she relented. "It's true. Everyone's already down there, just waiting on you."

Her best friend wrapped her deceptively strong hand around Sutton's and tugged. "Come on. We have time."

"Not too much time." She reluctantly took a few steps before she looked down at herself. "I need to change."

But she was only pulled harder, forcing her to walk as Emma's strength was added to Regan's.

"You said yourself we don't have too much time. It takes you forever to perfectly put your dress back."

Sutton only rolled her eyes again before she allowed them to pull her out of the room. Her bridal party was made up of Regan, Emma, Alex, Alia, with her sisters-in-law, Isla and Jane, to complete the ensemble.

Charlotte had chuckled teasingly at her when they'd worked out who would stand up with them. "Are you taking this time to show you have more friends than I do?"

Caleb and Dean were, of course, in her own bridal party. Along with her oldest brother William. And then Sutton's three brothers to even everything out.

"If Alison or Amanda," the top wedding planner in the city that Elizabeth and Alison had nabbed for them, "Catch us, Charlotte won't have a bride tomorrow," she whispered as they walked through the den, toward the east wing patio doors.

"They won't, you chicken. Their rooms are on the other side of this place." Regan shot back as Emma opened the back doors and ushered her out into the small rose garden.

And she came to a stumbling stop, breath leaving her in a gasp as surprise exploded inside of her.

The rose garden had been transformed since earlier this afternoon. Fairy lights were strung, illuminating it with an ethereal glow, the flowers looking somehow full to bursting. Less than twenty of the chairs their guests were supposed to sit in tomorrow were lined up in two small, intimate rows.

And standing thirty feet in front of her, on the far side of the patio, was Charlotte.

Surrounded by the blossoming roses, her fiancée locked eyes with her, a slow, crooked smile sliding onto her face. She looked simultaneously proud and amazed and… and Sutton felt like the breath was stolen right from her lungs as she stared. *God.*

Or… goddess, actually.

Because that's exactly what Charlotte looked like. Her dress with one strap over the shoulder, the material light and airy, revealing her collarbones and then delving between her breasts. It rained down her body in such a deceptively simple design, hugging slightly at her waist before flowing to the ground.

Sutton could literally feel her breath tremble out of her, barely able to take her eyes off of Charlotte to stare dumbly at Regan.

"I – what…" There were no words to express the racing thoughts in her mind. *Was this happening?* "What did you do?" She managed to get out.

Regan smoothed her hair over her shoulders as she shook her head. "My job was to get you here without suspecting a thing. I did it flawlessly. But your wife did the rest." She leaned up on her tiptoes and her best friend's soft lips brushed against her cheek. "Now go get married."

That strong hug minutes ago – which now felt like hours ago – made so much more sense now.

She linked hands with Emma and stepped back and gestured to Sutton's left, where she realized with a daze, her father was standing. With no idea where he came from or if he'd been there the entire time, she met his gentle smile with a teary one of her own.

Still reeling from the shock of it all, unable to wrap her mind around the fact that this was happening *now*, she took the arm he offered.

"This… is real." She made eye contact with her siblings and her mother, who was wiping the tears from her eyes already, as they walked forward.

"It's real," he confirmed in a whisper as he reached his other hand up to rub over the back of hers. "You got yourself a good one."

"The best one," she corrected firmly, as firmly as one could while living in a dream, as her eyes fell on Charlotte again.

She seemed to glow, herself. Luminescent in the twilight, her smile brighter than the moon itself.

Her dad pressed a kiss to her forehead, whispering, "I love you, honey."

It was all she could do to nod in response as Charlotte reached out for her, lacing their fingers together. She clung tightly, staring in wonder as she shook her head.

"I – but – why…" Any end to her sentence was overtaken by the sheer overwhelmed feeling inside.

Charlotte squeezed her hand, reassuring and stable as always. "I know my family threw a wrench into everything, but I want you to have what you want." Sutton slowly turned her head to look back at Charlotte. She could feel the tears – overwhelmed, stunned, and in love, *so in love* – brimming in her eyes and trying to blink them away only made them fall.

"I want you. That's all." It was true. Their wedding, no matter the spectacle it turned into, only mattered because it was for them.

It was only as Charlotte squeezed her hands again that she realized belatedly, "Your hands are shaking."

She looked down at them. Those perfect hands, the ones that knew her body like no one else, the ones Charlotte loves to gently trace over her jaw before going to work so they could hold the weight of the world.

"In excitement," Charlotte murmured, her voice nothing but soothing. "I want you, too, Sutton."

Dean stepped up, squeezing her shoulder as he passed. "With the power vested in me by the states of both Virginia and New York, are you ladies ready to begin?"

She knew Dean was speaking. She knew everyone she cared about most in the world was watching. She *knew* all of these things, but all she was truly aware of was Charlotte.

The way Charlotte stared at her as if she was the only thing that mattered, the solid feeling of her warm fingers interlaced with her own, the way her golden brown eyes gleamed as they never moved from Sutton's own for an instant.

She was *getting married* to Charlotte Thompson. In a moonlit garden, cocooned by the people who loved them the most, and this was it. This was all that mattered, really.

"Your vows, Sutton?" Was the only thing she truly registered from Dean, after… she didn't even know how long it had been since they'd begun.

For a brief moment, she panicked that she didn't have the vows she'd painstakingly worked on for weeks. But as she held Charlotte's gaze with her own, her heart flip-flopped in her chest and she realized that she didn't need them. Not really.

"I've dreamed about my wedding ever since I was a little girl. I know it's not a secret," she admitted, a bashful smile tugging at her lips as she looked down. She always thought she'd be more anxious than this, just by virtue of the occasion. But there was nothing inside of her except for a visceral *rightness*. "But I've dreamed of this moment a thousand times, at least."

"I never knew who the person in those dreams would be. I never knew how old I would be or what my career would be. None of those variables were ever clear. Nothing was, except that I was always… happy." She bit her lip, but even then it was unable to contain the smile that broke out on her face.

Her throat burned with the tears, the good ones that came from the never-ending well of sheer happiness brimming inside of her, her voice raw with truth as she confessed. "I could have existed in those worlds, a different me with a different someone else in a different life. But I know without a doubt I could live in a thousand lifetimes and still never be as happy as this one with you."

She knew she shouldn't have been surprised, but she was when Regan appeared next to her with the ring. A ring that was full of promises, ones she intended to keep for the rest of her life, as she slid it onto Charlotte's finger.

When she looked back at Charlotte, her eyes were brimming with tears. The most steadfast woman she'd ever known, with tears in her eyes as she took a deep breath and flexed her hands as she began speaking.

"I was never someone who dreamed about this." Charlotte confessed in the least shocking revelation with a self-deprecating smile. That then morphed into a thoughtful frown. "I didn't ever think I would find someone whose happiness would become more important than anything in the entire world."

She shook her head slightly, her perfectly curled hair bouncing as she searched Sutton's face, a smile taking hold. "But here you are and… you've changed me. Now, I am someone who dreams about getting married." Charlotte glanced down, her breath leaving her in a heavy tremble, honesty and sincerity written all over her features. "I want to marry you tonight, in front of our friends and family. And I want to marry you tomorrow in front of the entire world. I want this with you, Sutton, forever."

The luckiest woman in the universe, she thought, as she watched Charlotte slide a perfectly sized ring on her finger. It was all she could think, as she stared back at her *wife*. "I'll take forever and a day."

***

CNN || *Breaking News*
03 Nov 26

Charlotte Thompson wins New York Senate seat against incumbent democrat Sean O'Malley. O'Malley was running for re-election after having served his first term from '20-present. Thompson, granddaughter of Elizabeth Thompson, has worked with Mayor Dean Walker and served two terms in the House of Representatives.

"Sean O'Malley has done great work in the last few years, but it's time to push the boundaries even more," Thompson stated in her speech earlier this afternoon.

※※※

The New Yorker Recommends
December 28 2026

As an avid fan of Katherine Spencers' Honor Within series since the publication of Gates of Glass over a decade ago, I admit I was nervous about this installment being co-written with her daughter. I was wrong. It might be Sutton Spencer's first major publication, but her writing was just as sharp, enthralling, and poignant as her mother's. Hopefully there will be more from her in the future.

Part 5

The first time Sutton mentioned having children after they were married, it was six months after their wedding, and it hadn't been very serious. Well, it hadn't been not serious, either, but it hadn't been a *discussion*.

They'd gone on a short trip to Boston and Sutton had cradled Oliver and Jane's two-month-old son on her lap, making soft, gentle sounds at him. He'd blinked sleepily up at her with eyes so blue they nearly matched Sutton's exactly, and in all honesty, it was entirely precious.

"It's like you have a little baby mirror." She'd commented, hesitantly stroking a finger over his barely there hair.

Sutton's smile was bright and full as she'd looked at Charlotte. "I hope ours have your eyes," she'd whispered as she continued bouncing him in her arms.

Charlotte had *rolled* her eyes in response even as a pleased flare set off in her chest, as it always did when Sutton looked at her with that adoration. "Please, darling, it's practically a requirement for every baby to have these blue eyes."

The subject hadn't been brought up again until a year after their wedding. Charlotte had just become senator and they were putting some serious thought into upsizing from her condo to a house.

House hunting, despite starting a new avenue in her career and the fact that it was difficult to find a home they both liked, that fit their specifications, and was within reasonable distance to everywhere they frequently needed to go, in Manhattan wasn't the easiest task. But she'd found, despite the at times stressful aspects of it, that she rather enjoyed it.

Even if she was still pushing to hold out for another year or so; her grandmother's plan to retire from the office was looming and Charlotte happened to know that when her grandmother retired, she also planned to move to a smaller, more manageable home, rather than the sprawling penthouse she'd resided in for as long as Charlotte could remember.

And Charlotte wanted to make that *their* home.

Her hand was tangled with Sutton's as they trailed through the fourth house they'd toured and she could feel her wife's energy buzzing between them. Despite the fact that Charlotte was critical, she felt herself smiling at Sutton's ramble, as she tried to convince her they should buy this house.

"I know you want to buy your grandmother's place, and, I mean, it's a beautiful home; you know I wouldn't mind living there. But that's years away, babe, and that's only *if* she decides to move right after her retirement. Have you met your grandmother? She's not the most prone to change."

She couldn't help but roll her eyes even as she chuckled and squeezed her wife's hand in an amused reproach. "I've met her once or twice," she drawled. "But I happen to know she plans on moving fairly quickly. Besides, darling, two years isn't very long. Do you have such a big need to get out of our current home by then?"

It was clear in the way Sutton had slowed down, head turned to peer into a bathroom, that she was distracted even before she answered, "It's not like I *want* to leave." She brought up the hand that wasn't holding Charlotte's to stroke over the paint on the doorway, "I mean, it's our home," she added absently, but even so, with an affection in her voice that made Charlotte smile. "But there's only one guest room and it's hardly big enough."

Her eyebrows furrowed together in confusion. "Big enough?" She wracked her mind for what in the world Sutton could mean by that. "Are we hosting any long-term guests I've forgotten about?"

The only person who even semi-regularly stayed in that room was Regan, and she hadn't had any complaints in the past few years on the odd nights she spent there.

If Sutton's attention hadn't been clearly captured elsewhere, Charlotte knew her exasperation would have been far more intense than it was as she said, "Big enough for the kids."

She said it so nonchalantly that if Charlotte didn't know any better, she would have thought Sutton was already pregnant. The words brought Charlotte to a quick stop, though, and her stomach clenched uncomfortably as her heart leapt, because *the kids* – stopped her in her tracks.

And even after their house hunt was resolved – they did purchase that brownstone on the Upper West Side – the topic continued to get brought up more and more often over the following few months.

Whenever they saw their various nieces and nephews, even when they saw advertisements for baby items. And every time, Charlotte felt an uncontrollable shot of nerves through her entire body, and she thanked God that she was so practiced at evading and changing topics.

Though perhaps she wasn't as skilled as she thought she was, she thought ruefully, as she sighed and stared at the dark bedroom ceiling, her lips pursing together, as she tried to ignore this dreadful feeling in the pit of her stomach.

Because changing the subject was what had led her to this: laying in her and Sutton's bed… without Sutton in it.

She could count the amount of times that they hadn't slept together ever since having moved in together. When she was on trips to D.C. or other states, sometimes around the world, but Sutton was busy and couldn't attend with her. When Sutton took short visits back to see her family or sometimes long weekend trips with Regan.

Those were all markedly longer spans in time that she went without Sutton next to her when she fell asleep, considering that this was one night.

This was *one night* and despite the fact that she was bone tired, she couldn't rest.

Because all she could think about was the fact that Sutton was choosing to sleep in the guest room. *Away from me*, she self-corrected, biting hard into her bottom lip and closing her eyes as the backs of them burned.

No matter whenever they'd had little disagreements in the past years, it had never been bad enough to drive Sutton actually away from her. Not once had they chosen to sleep apart.

Not until this evening, that is.

Charlotte had only just walked through the door and poured herself a drink, only to undignifiedly choke on it and very nearly spit it back up. But she couldn't help it, with the sheer alarm that seemed to permeate through her.

Because the first thing Sutton said to her was. "I found some good places we could use to look for donors."

"Donors? That's –" she'd had to pause to cough, her heart beating wildly in her chest, "– a bit fast."

"I knew that would at least get a response," Sutton's voice had come low and triumphant but heated. Heated, like a simmer waiting to become a full-on boil. "I haven't looked yet, I obviously wouldn't do that without you." Sutton had bit her lip, eyes carefully watching Charlotte and she knew her wife could see right through anything she could try to project in that moment. "But I needed *something* to get your attention before you could change the subject."

She wanted to smile – almost – at the fact that of course Sutton would know, no matter how artful she was. Sutton knew her better than that. Every single day when she went to work there was always a polish she had to wear that she'd perfected years ago. It was a necessity, to make people only see what she needed them to see.

She knew now how incredible it was to be able to come home and not have any of that mask, any polished exterior, because she had someone to come home to who could see all of her.

But she couldn't smile, because god… having a baby, felt so daunting. In a hard to take a deep breath, stomach is filled with nerves kind of way that she was so unfamiliar with. After not only fantasizing about but planning on ruling one of the most powerful countries in the world one day, feeling daunted was not something she often felt.

She'd froze in place, entirely unsure of what to say and not wanting to look up from her drink to see her sweet Sutton's face as she'd swallowed hard, her voice measured, "I'm not sure it's the right time, for this conversation."

But of course, she hadn't been able to help looking up, just in time to see Sutton's face scrunch up in confusion. "Okay, but when is it going to be the right time? Because I've been wanting to talk about it for…" She'd played with the ends of her hair, before shrugging, "A while."

"I know," she'd answered, unable to pretend she hadn't heard the many conversation starters in the last couple of months. Her shoulders tensed, with this feeling brewing in her stomach that was heavy and made her almost feel sick. Of course she'd known; she knew Sutton almost better than she knew herself.

Her wife had tilted her head, a small, teasing smile playing on her lips. "Well, I'm not saying we need to go out and figure out baby names right now. I understand if you aren't ready yet, I know it's a big thing," her voice was so soft, in the way she had, that patient way. "But… I'm thirty-two, Charlotte. You're thirty-five. Even if we aren't going to have our first baby for a year or so, we need to plan it."

"I'm not sure it's the right time," she'd managed again as her chest seized in a panic she was entirely unfamiliar with.

Sutton let out a baffled laugh. "Not the right time? You plan more than anyone I've ever met," she assessed and it was entirely true. "You *love* making plans for the future –"

She did love planning, loved having a timeline and steps she would be following. It was methodical and satisfying, and she loved being able to see how close she was to a goal or an endgame.

But the thought of planning this was terrifying. How did she plan for something like this, when she was so unsure?

"– So, I figured we could make a whole night out of it," her wife's voice had been so hopeful, it hurt. "We can have dinner and I have all of these websites bookmarked, and…" She trailed off, the exuberance in her voice slowly leeching out before she tilted her head and gave Charlotte a long look. "And, you don't want to do this tonight."

Her voice was soft and questioning but *sure*, because she knew, and the somewhat crestfallen look on her face made Charlotte's stomach twist even more. She hated when Sutton wore anything even relating to that look, let alone being part of the cause.

She'd leaned back against the counter, a sigh breaking from her lips as she tried to find the right words to explain herself fully. Which was difficult, so difficult, because how was she supposed to do that when she knew that the thoughts swirling in her head would break Sutton's heart?

She apparently hadn't had to say anything, though, before those all too perceptive blue eyes had narrowed up at her. "Do you want to do this… *any* night?"

"I don't know." The admittance had left her quickly, emotionally, her voice feeling raw. But the worst part was that she could actually see the way the words hit Sutton like a blow.

From there, the entire evening had gone downhill. Well, more downhill.

She could so easily picture the way Sutton had blanched, the way she crumpled back in her chair in surprise, before that had seeped into a rare anger.

"But… we've talked about it," she'd said, her voice low and hurt and betrayed in a way Charlotte had never heard aimed at her. "Years ago. You said – we agreed that was in our future."

Which was true. When they were dating, when they'd gotten more sure and more serious – even though if Charlotte was honest, she didn't know if she and Sutton were ever *not* serious –they'd laid out what they wanted in their lives, and determined if they'd want it all together.

It had been done in soft voices, intermittent with a lot of laughter, even more kissing, and Charlotte staring at Sutton and feeling like she saw the world as an even more expansive, glorious universe reflecting back at her.

That universe for Sutton included having kids.

And the thing was, Charlotte would have to be both dumb and blind if she thought at any point that Sutton didn't want children, even if they'd never had any sort of conversation about it. And she was certainly neither of those things.

Her wife practically turned into a pile of mush every time she saw a baby in public; she'd done so long before they'd even considered getting married. Likely for long before they'd even met. They now had eight nieces and nephews and not only did Sutton adore them and love spending as much time with all of them as possible, but she was *good* at it – at being with them. Soothing them, making them laugh.

Babies – and toddlers, and children; all of the young ones in their extended family – loved Sutton, too. It was as though she had a magic touch.

And there, in those soft moments when it was just the two of them away from everything in the world, when having children with Sutton was a thought for the undetermined future, it felt… nice. During those moments in their relationship when they'd talked about their future and children had come up, it hadn't been hard to think that she would want them, too.

But, she'd realized in the last few months, that there was a startling difference between the dreamy undetermined future babies with thoughts of a baby with red hair and blue eyes in a world that only existed with their little family, and the actuality of her wife wanting to truly, actually bring a life into this very real, demanding world with her.

"I'm sorry," her words had come out in a whisper. "But there are other things to think about, now."

There was *so much* to think about.

It had been the wrong thing to say though. Especially when Sutton had stood up and wrapped her arms around herself, looking hurt and angry and it spiraled to the point that she couldn't stop thinking about now as she laid in bed hours later –

Sutton staring at her, eyes wide after all of her seeds of doubt about ever having a child in the future came out and moments of silence sat heavy between them. "That would have been nice to know years ago."

Which, what did that *mean*? She wasn't entirely sure, but she knew it made her stomach leap in fear.

Before she could even figure out what to say, Sutton had shaken her head. "I just… I need some time to think."

That had been at seven this evening and now it was – she spared a look at her phone on the bedside table, pursing her lips – almost three in the morning. Eight hours of silence.

There had been many times in their lives together that they existed in comfortable silence in the evenings. Working either side by side or in separate rooms, or relaxing and decompressing to just *be* together.

They'd never existed in a tenseness like this. She'd never been met with a quiet goodnight when she'd tentatively informed her wife that she was going to go to bed. It took everything inside of her to not go into the guest room and… she didn't know. Do something just get Sutton to talk to her.

She had to be up for work in three hours, she'd *been* up for over twenty hours, and she couldn't sleep. Not when she felt like this. Not when the most solid thing in her life, her marriage, felt like it was at the closest to fraying that it had ever been.

The back of her throat felt thick and scratchy, and she didn't think there had been a time where she'd been more upset in their marriage than she was at that moment.

Exactly how much time would her wife need to think? Because Charlotte was itching with everything she *was* to go to her now, even if she didn't know quite how to make sense in words – at least, words that wouldn't break Sutton's heart.

But Charlotte didn't do anything by halves; when she wanted something, she wanted it with everything she had. And the very specific *thing* she couldn't get over about having a baby was… a big one.

She turned onto her side, only getting more agitated as she couldn't get comfortable like that, either.

If she couldn't get comfortable for one night like this, what was she going to do if –

She froze entirely as the bedroom door opened, before her body melted in relief. Charlotte wasn't facing the door but she didn't have to be to know the soft footsteps approaching the bed; she could place them anywhere.

And she thought it was much in the same way that Sutton didn't have to see her in the dark to know that she wasn't sleeping as she slipped under the covers, settling naturally into her place in their bed. "Just because I can't sleep without you doesn't mean I'm not upset."

She knew her wife meant those words, but… she couldn't help but feel reassurance flowing through her veins, her shoulders untensing just at feeling Sutton climbing into bed with her.

"It doesn't mean that I don't feel like you lied to me," Sutton added, and the pain and anger in her voice was impossible to mistake. It felt like a knife to the stomach. "Because I know that haven't kids isn't for everyone, but you *said* it was what you wanted, too. I've been thinking about this for a long time," she confessed, as if it was a secret. "And I've had so many ideas and possibilities to talk to you about. So, now, I feel –"

Her voice seemed to break, bleeding from anger to sadness in a way that twisted the knife. "Like you've been avoiding this and dodging having to talk about it, and I can't remember the last time you've done that, and I just…"

She trailed off, her voice wobbling and Charlotte couldn't stand to hear it. Even though Sutton was upset, she didn't know if she had it in her to listen to Sutton feel so desolate and not do *anything*. Even if she was the cause.

Twisting, she propped herself up on her elbow as she slid her other hand out instinctively to reach for her wife. Who was laying on her back, biting her lip hard as she clearly tried to reign control over her emotions. Her eyes were dark and shining with tears, but her jaw was set in the way that told Charlotte in no uncertain terms was she angry.

It was that last part that stopped her hand as soon as her fingertips brushed over Sutton's tank top. Instead, her eyes trailed over her wife's face, her heart in her throat, and there were many things she wanted to say. But what came out surprised them both, "I didn't lie to you."

Sutton's forehead furrowed momentarily in confusion, before she shook her head. "But you – you said before that you wanted this, and now you don't –"

"I did mean it. And sometimes I do think about it. About having a baby," she interrupted, her own heart leaping into her throat at the admission, and her fingers twitched where they were against Sutton's side, wanting to take hold of her sleep shirt and relish in the feeling of her. "I didn't lie to you but I... I have been avoiding it." It took everything inside of her to force out, "Because I'm scared."

The words, the *truth*, hung between them and perhaps dodging the topic was easier, but it wasn't possible now. Especially not when she could *see* how much it hurt Sutton.

That heat, that anger, seemed to melt away minutely right before her eyes, as Sutton stared at her. Charlotte's gaze dipped as she took a deep breath through her nose and held it, focusing on the tendrils of red hair that had escaped Sutton's loose ponytail and instead touched over her collarbone.

She hated that admission. For many reasons, but more than anything because while she didn't have to put on a brave face in front of Sutton, she knew her wife viewed many of her actions as fearless. And Charlotte liked it; she loved the way Sutton looked at her when she prevailed against anything that could possibly deter them.

It had been over six years since she'd come out to the public and that had been the last time she'd been *so* afraid of anything. And this... this fear felt ever more overwhelming than that had. So much harder to explain.

"What are you afraid of?" There was surprise and genuine curiosity in Sutton's tone.

Charlotte wasn't sure at what point in their relationship that was all it took to coax her into almost anything, but here they were. Despite the unsettled feeling still curling in her stomach, she tilted her head to look back into her eyes. "Recently, I..." Her voice shook and she pressed her fingers into the mattress for stability to admit, "I'm afraid that if having kids isn't going to work out, that I'll lose you. And I couldn't bear to lose you."

The words were thick with tears that she didn't want to allow to fall. Instead, she turned her face to rub at the fist she used to prop her head up, wiping them away before they could properly exist.

And the hand she'd left at Sutton's side was immediately covered by her wife's, the warmth encompassing her own, with the slight jut of her wedding and engagement bands a bit colder and all the more comforting for its familiarity.

"You're never going to lose me." Her assurance was strong and immediate, and it loosened that knot in Charlotte's chest, her breath leaving her on a long exhale.

She squeezed her hand hard, feeling Sutton there with her for a long moment, before she forced herself to speak the thoughts – the insecurity – that had taken root inside of her months ago. "I'm worried." She squeezed Sutton's hand a little harder to get the strength she needed. "That I'm going to be a bad mother."

There. There it was.

And by worried, she truly meant terrified. Because she was fairly certain she already knew.

"What?" The sincere disbelief in Sutton's voice was almost a comfort and she knew even before she turned to look at her what she would look like. With blue eyes wide, shaking her head. "You'd be such an amazing mom, Charlotte."

There was such a certainty in her voice that she so desperately *wanted* to agree. Because she could make plans for entire cities, countries, even, and be sure that she was doing the right thing. But not with this.

"No, *you* will be an amazing mom," she corrected, her gaze searching Sutton's while her stomach twisted.

Because Sutton had an innate sweetness, an innate sense of nurturing, that Charlotte couldn't replicate in the least.

"Your mother is… supermom," she settled on, rolling her eyes at herself, but it was so true. "She's the epitome of what a mom should be and you have all of those same –" She vaguely gestured at her wife with the hand she'd been propping her head up on, before she pushed herself to sit up next to Sutton against the headboard. "– perfect mom qualities and you aren't even a mother, yet!"

Sutton was already shaking her head, the fingers threaded through Charlotte's holding tighter as she opened her mouth, but Charlotte shook her head to stop her.

"Please, just…" She took in a deep breath, because it had taken her months to get to this point, and she couldn't stop now. "Look at my mother. At both of my parents. I spent more time in my childhood with my nanny than either of them, with how busy they were. By the time I was fourteen, I saw my parents twice a week."

And that was on a good week, she silently added with a scoff, even as she felt her hands shake a little. It wasn't even that she resented her childhood or wished her parents were different; she hadn't even wished it at the time. She hadn't known anything else. It felt – fine. Normal.

"They were off running their businesses and I didn't miss them, Sutton." She implored her wife to understand something that only in her mid-thirties seemed to be making an appearance in her psyche. "I don't miss them, now, when I only see them a few times a year. We're all busy and that's perfectly fine for all of us."

When it came to the person who had shaped her the most, it was undoubtedly her grandmother, and even then… the vulnerability that seemed to choke her though, and she couldn't add anything onto her thoughts.

Sutton's thumb brushed softly over her knuckles, before she felt her shift and her warm body was pressed against Charlotte's side. "Your parents aren't bad people. And even so, you aren't them."

She closed her eyes at the feeling of Sutton pressing her soft lips in a lingering kiss against her shoulder. "No, they aren't bad people and they love me in their own way," she agreed, her breathing feeling a little shallow, before she shook back her hair and looked at her wife. "But they were busy and absent and they raised us as if that was normal. Which was fine for me. But it's not the parent I want to be."

The kind I'm positive I would be, hung unsaid but they both knew it.

Sutton's forehead crinkled in that earnest way she had, as she looked up at Charlotte from where she propped herself up. And she lifted her hand up to rub her thumb softly over that spot in the center of her forehead, even as a humorless laugh left her.

"And I know you're going to say I won't be and that you'll truly believe that," she murmured, feeling this *love* for Sutton and her staunch belief in her sit comfortably in her chest. But she couldn't bring herself to agree with her, even if she wished she could. "But how can I not be absent? It's already hard to balance schedules, even with just you and I."

They always did their best to make time for one another. But since becoming a senator, her hours had gotten longer, work just that step more intense, and they already had to plan events, travel, and special occasions months in advance.

Her stomach twisted with the thought, as she bit at the inside of her lip and trailed her eyes over Sutton's face slowly, stroking her hand down her cheek. "And what about future elections? The presidency? If I get elected –"

"When," Sutton interrupted, nudging her face softly against her, pressing more firmly against Charlotte's hand.

Even though she was being serious and trying to truly explain her fears, she couldn't help but grin at that, "If I get elected," she continued, "That's even less time I'll have. And then what?" She slid her fingers down Sutton's jaw, tipping her chin up. "You'll be an amazing mother, but what happens when I just can't do it all? You're left having the weight of raising our kids without me being there. I can't…" she cut herself off. "I *won't* do that to you."

Her insecurities spilled out between them and she had to swallow back this ache that settled in the back of her throat at it all.

"What happens when I fail them?" She whispered. *What if I fail you?* She just *couldn't* bear to do that.

"You won't," Sutton assured her and the sheer *belief* was so intense in her voice, even as her voice was soft. "I have faith in you."

Her eyes fluttered closed at the soothing sound of her voice as she let out a quiet, teasing chuckle. "You always have faith in me."

It never seemed to matter what the subject was; Sutton never faltered. Even when perhaps she should.

"And I haven't been wrong yet," she countered, tapping Charlotte's bare thigh just where her pajama shorts ended, as if to emphasize her point.

Sutton pulled away, pushing herself up to sit right across from her.

"We don't have to have kids," Sutton said, her voice firm and Charlotte could hear the longing in the mere word. Her hands down Charlotte's arms to settle in her palms. "But if this fear is what's holding you back, then… we can go slow. I just need you to *talk to me*," she finished with a plea.

She slid her hands out from under Sutton's, cupping her wife's jaw and tugging her in pressing a lingering, soft kiss to her mouth. Sutton's skin was so warm under her fingertips and it was their first proper kiss all day long and *god*, she hadn't realized how much she needed it.

"I promise," she whispered as they pulled back, pressing their foreheads together as she felt those pieces of her that had been in utter unrest settle into their proper place.

"Now," Sutton breathed, her eyes closed as her forehead nudged into Charlotte's. "Can we lay down? Because I couldn't even pretend to get comfortable in the guest bed. And maybe… we could talk more about this tomorrow?"

"Yes, darling." She could hear the relief in her own voice and it only mirrored a small fraction of what felt broken wide open and vulnerable inside of her. "Tomorrow sounds good."

She dipped her head to press another kiss against Sutton's lips, to get another quick taste and that feeling, before Sutton laid back in their bed. She grabbed Charlotte's hand to tug her down as well. Not that it took much convincing, really.

She pressed her cheek to Sutton's chest, stroking her hand over her hip. Before she slowly slid over that soft, warm skin so that her fingertips brushed over her lower stomach. A baby. She turned her face enough to press a kiss to Sutton's shoulder softly, breathing her in, as she stroked her fingertips over her stomach again.

"I think having a little you would be…" She trailed off, her hushed voice breaking into the night, narrowing her eyes as she pictured it, pictured that little baby with bright red hair and those blue eyes. And if there was anything good in this world, they would light up the same way Sutton's did when she laughed. "Better than words can describe."

The muscles in Sutton's stomach flexed under her hand as she felt Sutton inhale deeply. "Really?" The hope in her voice was unmistakable.

The niggling worry inside of her didn't disappear completely, but it was quieter now. "Really."

***

People's Exclusive First Look!
27 Jan 2028

Charlotte and Spencer Thompson have been notoriously tight-lipped regarding their daughter since her birth last April. People has the exclusive first official pictures released to the public and interview with the new parents.

People: *With so many incredible women in your lives, was your daughter's name inspired by anyone in particular?*
S: *Actually, no. We spent the months leading up to her being born disagreeing about names. It started becoming a game – the first thing we would say when we saw one another every day was a new name. And we would just laugh and move on, because we could never agree one on that seemed just right.*
C: *Then one day while we were watching TV, we heard Madelyn and just – looked at each other. That was it.*
S: *We actually did plan to give her the middle name Elizabeth, after Charlotte's grandmother, originally. But ended up going with Regan, after our best friend.*
People: *Interesting choice. I sense a story there?*
C: *God, is there ever. Madelyn was determined to make her mark on this world –*
S: *Just like her mother.*
C: *[laughing] Okay, fine, I will accept responsibility for that. Anyway, she wasn't due for three weeks and I was in a conference in D.C. but she went into labor early.*
S: *God, it was terrifying. My mom was supposed to be here and Charlotte had cleared out of city travel for two weeks before. My best friend rushed me to the hospital and, well,*

Madelyn did not want to wait. So she was with me through the delivery.

People: *You weren't there?*

C: I arrived just in time for Madelyn to be born.

S: She crashed into the room, chased by security, looking absolutely crazed –

C: There was a cab driver outside parked half on the sidewalk who made a hefty tip that day. When I remembered to send someone out to pay him. For the next one, I'm not leaving the city for an entire month beforehand.

S: [staring at Charlotte] The next one?

C: [grinning] Yeah. The next one.

Part 6

"*God*, yes, d-don't stop," she panted the words out into the darkness of their bedroom, her back arching as Charlotte thrust even harder into her.

Fuck, her wife used a strap-on like it was a seamless extension of her body, and Sutton wasn't even quite sure she could feel her legs anymore, her mouth falling open as pleasure screamed through her body.

Her nails dug hard into her wife's back and she still had just enough presence of mind to register Charlotte's deep groan against her neck. Before she bit down against her, right where her neck met her shoulder, the spot that her wife always seemed to come back to. The slight pain flashed white behind her eyes, only making her throb even more, needing Charlotte to take her harder.

Charlotte's hands gripped at where Sutton's knees were locked around her hips, pushing them back so she could thrust even deeper and –

The moan that broke from her mouth at the shifting angle came from somewhere deep inside of her, somewhere that could only *feel* as Charlotte's hands fell onto the pillow on either side of her head, her body laying over Sutton's, and her wife's hard nipples rubbing against her own sent shockwaves through her body right to her clit.

Her wife's mouth closed hot around her earlobe, before she felt her teeth bite down, and Sutton swore her entire body was on fire. The groan she let out into her ear was deep and needy and the knowledge that she was so wet Sutton *knew* she was dripping onto her thighs even though she also knew it wasn't enough friction for her to come.

"I love this," Charlotte's voice was so low and raspy in her ear, and her hips jerked harder against the slim ones pounding into her at the sound of it. "I could feel you like this, *mm*, a thousand times and it'll never be enough."

She clenched tighter, her toes curling, and there was no way in the world that she would be able to stop the desperate moans she could feel more than hear leaving the back of her throat.

She was so close, so close, "So close," she gasped, raking her nails down Charlotte's back, her hips straining up against Charlotte's even as Charlotte's hips started to snap against her, before pressing in and, "Ch-Charlo…tte," her voice trembled with the white hot heat that was ratcheting up inside of her, pulling everything tighter and tighter, her legs starting to shake.

Yes, yes, god yes, the way Charlotte slid into her deeply, grinding their hips together, was just what she – just what she needed. The perfect way, the way she needed to come, before Charlotte's hand slid between them, and everything inside of Sutton trembled on the brink, knowing what was going to happen.

The second Charlotte's thumb brushed over her clit, her back bowed sharply, her mouth falling open as the heat that coiled so tightly inside of her burst out, and all she could feel was pleasure.

She swore that she whited out from it, the blood rushing in her ears, while her body throbbed and she could hardly breathe. Her hips arched hard off the bed, pressing up into Charlotte's, wrapping her arms as tight as she could around her to steady herself, letting herself get swept away.

Sutton couldn't be sure but she knew it was actual minutes later when she fully came back to herself.

Actual minutes, before she was left panting to catch her breath her limbs feeling so heavy and full like they always did after sex. She whined softly in the back of her throat when she felt Charlotte slowly, gently pull out of her, leaving her pleasantly sated and sore.

Her eyes closed, taking in the immediate aftermath feeling, for only a few moments before she heard the dull *thud* that was unmistakably her wife taking off the strap-on. And blue eyes fluttered open to see Charlotte crawling back toward her on the bed.

There was a flush over her skin, gorgeous and luminous even in the dark room, her eyes dark and hungry and when she was close enough Sutton could see that her hand was very nearly shaking from how aroused she knew she was. She *knew* how worked up Charlotte got from fucking her like that; because she knew exactly how aroused she got when fucking Charlotte the same way.

The only difference was that the pressure against her clit and the rush of taking Charlotte over like that – and knowing that Charlotte wanted her to take over – made Sutton come.

She barely had her energy back, but she *needed* to make Charlotte come. She wanted to taste her, to feel her, to hear her fall apart, and she reached out for her. "Come up here."

All she had to do was gesture for Charlotte to know exactly what she meant. She shuffled down a bit on the bed, adjusting her neck and hair before nodding at Charlotte, feeling ravenous for the taste of her.

The nod was all Charlotte needed for encouragement, before she kneeled on either side of Sutton's head. God she didn't think that feeling of being surrounded by those soft thighs would ever not be the most arousing feeling in the world. "You're soaked," she murmured, both teasing and amazed as she licked her lips at the wetness that had, indeed, dripped onto her wife's thighs.

"Of course," Charlotte sighed, before a whine worked out of her throat. "I need you so much, I'm so close already."

The need in her voice made Sutton groan herself. "Hold onto the headboard," she whispered.

She stroked her hands up the outside of Charlotte's legs, feeling the trembling in her muscles, before she landed on those perfectly curved hips, holding her firmly for only a moment, before she pulled her down, attaching her mouth immediately to her hard clit, sucking firmly, before laving it with her tongue.

Blue eyes stayed open, staring up Charlotte's body to take in the utterly perfect way her back snapped back in an arch, her head thrown back with her mouth open in a silent scream. She could *feel* the laboring in her wife's breath already, as her hands tightened against the headboard.

Charlotte's hips moved without any encouragement, already jerky as Sutton stroked her with her tongue, moaning against her and reveling in the way the reverberations moved through Charlotte's body.

The thighs around her ears were already shaking, muffling the sounds falling from her wife's mouth into the room around them, and she tightened her hold, knowing just how much Charlotte liked it.

She slid her mouth down, licking into her entrance, pressing her tongue into Charlotte. The taste of her coated her mouth, her chin, her neck, and she whimpered at the feeling, needing to cross her own legs despite still feeling how well Charlotte had made her come.

Charlotte's hips started shaking, the walls around her tongue clenching harder, and even though the sounds were muffled, she knew Charlotte was panting out her name on repeat now. It lit her up like a match, *needing* to make Charlotte come for her, into her mouth.

She moved back up, taking Charlotte's clit between her lips and sucking with just the pressure she knew Charlotte loved, feeling the way her pussy clenched harder. Scratching her nails down shaking thighs, she dug in harder, moaning and flicking her tongue faster and faster over the hard nub, until Charlotte's hips jerked once, twice, and a third time pressed hard down into her as her head snapped forward on a groan.

She held the eye contact with Charlotte as she came, dripping into Sutton's mouth. Her shaking intensified before slowly coming to a stop, her breath panting into the room around them.

Carefully, knowing how sensitive her wife was, she slid her mouth down, licking around her as she felt Charlotte catch her breath above her, a dazed smile on her lips. Her hands fell from the headboard, stroking softly over the top of her head before she pushed off Sutton. Just enough to collapse next to her on the bed.

Sutton felt somewhat in a daze herself for a few long minutes, the blood rushing so pleasantly in her ears while she felt like her entire body was singing still – now feeling both lethargic and swimming with energy – and she hummed out a breath as she reached out to stroke her hand over Charlotte's back, just to feel her close.

Her fingertips moved over her wife's soft skin, able to feel the way her heart was still pounding in her chest, as she languidly stretched. "I still don't think I can feel my legs."

"Mm," Charlotte's voice rumbled in her chest, a little raspy even as the self-satisfaction in her tone was so clear. "That was the goal, darling."

"I didn't realize my being published would make you want to ravish me so much," she meant to tease, but the reality of the words still amazed her.

"I always want to ravish you. But what can I say?" Her grin turned sharp, the gleam in her eyes setting Sutton on fire as if she hadn't seen it thousands of times by now in their life together.

She pushed up to her side, running her eyes over her wife's body, taking in the gentle arch of her back, the flaring of her hips, the way her hair was tousled and messy over her shoulder. Light brown eyes glinted up at her with the smirk she saw on her wife's face more often than not.

Sutton was years beyond embarrassment at seeing Charlotte in her naked glory or being utterly bare in front of her in turn. She grinned indulgently down at her, the joy of the day still hardly sinking in.

Charlotte sighed, lightly and sated, before she pushed herself up to sit. Simultaneously, she reached one hand out behind her to find the water bottle she always kept next to the bed while the other pulled the sheet around her to ward off any possible chill in their bedroom.

Blue eyes traced over Charlotte's flushed cheeks as she sipped, and she knew in this moment that she was the luckiest woman in the country, if not the world.

Charlotte quirked an eyebrow as she handed her the water. "What are you smiling at?"

She accepted it, rubbing the lukewarm bottle between her hands. "Nothing. Just... I'm happy," she shook her head, her hair tickling a bit as it brushed against her back, as she took a long sip.

"Me too," Charlotte winked, before she leaned forward, the enthusiasm written all over her absolutely buzzing. "Now, tell me. Exactly what happened tonight."

"I tried to do that when I came home," she teased, kicking her foot out enough as she tugged their comforter over herself to nudge her wife's leg. "*Someone* got us distracted."

Charlotte waved her hand in the air as if sweeping away her statement. "Okay, so I may have been a bit… eager," she settled on, pursing her lips. "But in fairness to myself, you walked in the door, looking absolutely delicious in your dress, before telling me that your novel was going to be published. I want all of the details now."

The look in Charlotte's eyes was absolutely unrepentant and made her stomach pleasantly dip, knowing how incredibly fortunate they were that they could be married for eight years and that she still felt like this.

Still she scoffed, because that really *had* been about all she'd been able to say before her wife had somewhat pounced on her. But Sutton had had so much energy rolling off of herself in that moment, that she'd responded in equal fervor.

She took another sip of water. "First things first – how were the girls tonight?"

It was a very rare evening when Sutton wasn't home to put their daughters to bed and it was also one of her favorite times with the girls.

Madelyn, with her bright eyes and mischievous smile that somehow looked more like Charlotte's than her own in spite of genetics. Though she wasn't yet five, she was already becoming a master of talking her way into extra bedtime stories. And Sutton loved sitting on her daughter's plush horse-themed quilt and weaving together stories for her.

And now that Ellie was two, she was old enough to sit in either her or Charlotte's lap and actually listen to the tales as well. Her participation in bedtime was quieter than Madelyn's – golden brown-green eyes always blinking up in quiet attention as she cuddled close to whomever she was sitting with.

Charlotte's smile was immediate and so warm, it made everything inside of her melt. "Well, I held off on telling Madelyn three stories; she only talked her way into two tonight. And Wolfie's foot is probably going to have to be sewed on again." Her voice was tinged with amusement at the mention of Ellie's stuffed wolf whose left leg had needed surgery last year. "I did my best to keep him together for the night, but your sewing skill is going to be a necessity."

The love that shined through whenever their daughters were involved, even when she was utterly exasperated, sometimes still baffled Sutton that Charlotte had questioned how amazing a mother she would be.

"And I was informed by both girls that while mama has the better stories, your voices simply don't compare to mine," she tossed in, throwing her hair back in playful victory.

Sutton didn't have to be home earlier to know that Charlotte had probably cajoled and tickled both girls until they gasped out unapologetic apologies for the joking "who has better bedtime stories" debate that had been going on since Madelyn was old enough to understand what bedtime stories were.

She narrowed her eyes. "We'll see about that tomorrow."

Charlotte hummed, before tugging the blanket tighter around her shoulders, eyes gleaming. "Now, *tell me*, darling. The meeting."

The excitement that had been paired with nerves for the last couple of weeks leading up to the meeting returned with a vengeance, and she shook her head before she reached up to draw her hands through her hair. "I don't even know where to begin…"

She really didn't.

In truth, she hadn't really planned on this happening until it all just seemed to be *happening*. Everything about her novel had been rather unexpected.

She'd had thoughts before having the girls of possibly writing her own novel at some point in the future. But she'd been working at Hunter College full time and had been contemplating taking on a doctorate program, not to mention, well, being the wife of a very busy Senator. Who was both a public figure and was becoming known as a trailblazer when it came to how many projects she was involved in and leading.

In the past years, she would never say she'd developed even nearly the taste for the political game that her wife had. But she could say, now – finally – with confidence that when it came to involving herself in Charlotte's initiatives and campaigns that she'd found her own taste for them. And it was a time and energy consuming taste.

By the time they'd even conceived Madelyn, Sutton had already decided that she wouldn't go back to being a professor after her maternity leave until however many children they had were older. And likely not even then, if she was being honest with Charlotte's career trajectory.

Then Madelyn had been born, perfect and beautiful and time consuming. And by the time Madelyn was nearly two, they'd opted to use Charlotte's egg for her to carry their second baby, which had resulted in a more complicated pregnancy than her first.

But Ellie had been born just as perfect and beautiful and now doubly as time consuming with both girls. No matter how much Charlotte insisted that Sutton should go back to work if she wanted and that they would make it work – which, she knew that they *would* if that was what she wanted – she just… she knew it was the right thing for her to take that time off.

She did enjoy working as a literature professor and wouldn't have minded doing it as a legitimate career. But the thing that Charlotte just couldn't understand on a personal level given her own utter passion for her career, was that there was no burning desire inside of her for work.

She'd sated her need for doing something else beyond her family by collaborating with her mother. She co-wrote a book with her in her newest historical fiction series, she'd made an addition into one of the anthologies her mom's publishers had released – a whimsical, light romance. Those projects were smaller, helped her improve, and got her creativity flowing in a way that she felt thrilled by.

It was more than enough for her to be *happy*. She had her daughters, her wife, her family, her Regan, her occasional writing side work.

Then, though, Madelyn had started preschool and Ellie was so introspective – meeting all of her appropriate milestones and so responsive to the world around her, but seemed to take it all in with wide eyes and soft coos – and the free time she'd had seemed abundant. There was too much of it and not enough to do, and after a conversation with her mom, she'd started writing her own book.

It had taken only three months for her to write her novel and in that time, the only person who read it was Regan. Who somewhat demanded to read it as soon as Sutton would jot down ideas in her presence.

By the time she revealed it to Charlotte, the rough draft had been complete. And even though she knew she could have probably written utter garbage and Charlotte would never think so, she'd been nervous.

She'd been entirely unprepared for the way her wife's eyes had been wide and surprised when she'd finished devouring the draft. "*This* is what you've been working on?" She'd asked, sheer shock laced into her tone.

She'd felt sheepish, wondering what her mother was thinking now that she'd been sent the same copy. "Um. Yes? Do you – what do you think?"

Charlotte had been thoughtfully quiet for a few seconds, her voice contemplative. "I think I was expecting something… that you'd done before. Something like what you've worked on with your mother, or even some of those romantic tales you spin, and I know if you wrote either one of them, they would be incredible." A sly grin took over her face, admiration shining from her eyes. "I think I've been with you for so long and you still shock me."

The look had stolen her breath right out from her, feeling herself delight in the praise even as her cheeks flushed. "You think it's really good?"

Because the literal suspense novel that had ended up formulating in her mind when she'd sat down to write – intending to write just what her wife had thought she would be writing – had shocked even herself.

"I think," she'd begun slowly, approaching Sutton in a nearly predatory way. "That my wife is a damn genius."

After receiving similar praise from her mother and then the rest of her family and friends, she'd finally sent it to Nicholas after several weeks of her former mentor-turned-coworker-turned-friend demanding to see it.

From there, everything had gone so fast, leading up to tonight…

She took a deep breath. "Well, you know how Nicholas had sent it to his connection at the publishing house?"

In fact, Nicholas had promptly sent her novel off without telling her first in an entirely unsurprising move.

"Of course." Charlotte nodded, urging her on.

"Well…" She blew out that breath, her forehead furrowing as she ran over all of her thoughts, trying to process them. "I met with Kym, who's apparently one of the *executives*," she shook her head in disbelief. "And she said – well, she said that she'd accepted the novel because of her friendship with Nicholas and because, um, my name would garner interest no matter what." She bit her lip, thinking about how that comment had made her feel sick.

And with the way Charlotte's eyes set, looking like fire wove through them and the way her jaw set, she knew she was feeling the same thing. "She said that to you? She had to audacity –"

Quickly, she placed her hand on her wife's forearm, stroking the soft skin there as she interrupted, "Yes, she said that, but *then* she ended up quite… giddy." It was the only word she could think of to describe it. "And said that she actually genuinely loved the plot and the writing and the characters." The astonishment she'd felt at hearing those words from someone whose *job* it was to find, read, and publish some of the best novels that had been written in the last decade still sat wondrously on her shoulders.

She could feel the tension drain slightly from Charlotte. "Well, Sera," her main character. "Is quite like you. It's impossible not to love her."

She grinned, wide and unbelievably bashful, as she looked down at her lap, tucking her hair behind her ear. "Actually, she was based more on *you*." She cleared her throat before Charlotte would disagree with her, as she knew she would. "But she – she asked about the future ideas to follow up, and when I told her I only had just started coming together with outlines for the next part, she... she offered me a three book deal, with the first one to be expedited. I'm going to be on the shelf in less than a year." The amazement that rocked through her was echoed in her voice as she looked back up at Charlotte, eyes wide.

The loose deal had been drawn up over dinner, with the promise of a contract to be sent to her and Charlotte's lawyer to be reviewed within two weeks. And Sutton had ridden that high all the way home, up until she'd walked through the door, checked in both of her daughter's bedrooms to see them sound asleep, before telling Charlotte in breathless wonder. "They want to publish me."

Then had come... well, everything else.

She drew in a sharp breath as Charlotte quickly, smoothly leaned forward, surging up to her knees to cup Sutton's jaw and murmur, "I'm so proud of you."

The sheer, burning *love* that swept through her at the sincerity in her wife's eyes nearly took all of her breath away. Even before the rest was swept away in a yelp, as Charlotte pushed forward again, maneuvering her swiftly onto her back, a breathless laugh on her lips even as they both paused, automatically waiting to see if the sound had woken up the girls.

Her knees automatically came up to bracket Charlotte's hips as the silence of their home remained as much, and she grinned up at her wife. "We are so lucky that they both sleep like rocks."

"So incredibly lucky," Charlotte echoed, nuzzling her way down Sutton's neck. "We'll have to thank Isla for those strange mobiles she sent claiming to have sleep therapeutic powers one of these days."

"We didn't even hang them up." She giggled, thinking about the incredulous look on Charlotte's face when Isla had given them the hideous mobiles when she'd been pregnant with Madelyn, before turning her head into the pillow to muffle both her laugh and the gasping breaths she knew were sure to come.

She could feel her wife's smile against her. "Semantics, darling."

***

New York Times Bestseller List
20 Feb 2032

1. *A Touch of Truth* by Sutton Spencer

Two women. One disappearance. A million motives. And it seems no one really cares.

Except for her.

Seraphina Thorne never thought that when socialite Emilia Michaels asked her only weeks ago to write her life story, she would actually be writing the story of her presumed death. But when nothing adds up the way it should, she can't find it in herself to overlook the suspiciousness everyone else seems to simply accept.

In digging deeper Sera pieces together Emilia's past, what happened to her, and what's really the truth. The truth that someone will go to any lengths to keep hidden…

Praise for "A Touch of Truth"

"If you believe you know what you're getting into after reading Spencer's profound collaborations in Katherine Spencer's Honor Within series – guess again. Spencer – writing under her maiden name in homage to her literary roots – reaches a level that is entirely different: gripping and authentic with an adrenaline rushed plot and a heroine you can't help but root for." – The Washington Post

"Absolutely electrifying! Your heart will be pounding through the entire journey. The wait for the next book, The Rumor of Ruin, is going to be excruciating." – Publishers Weekly

"A masterful play on words that will seduce the reader within minutes. Filled with vividly depicted scenes, flawed and full characters, and nerve-ending cliffhangers, A Touch of Truth is nothing short of astonishing." – The Atlantic

Part 7

Charlotte wasn't entirely certain if it was her who was buzzing or if it was the entire energy of the building around her; perhaps it was a combination of both. She just knew that she knew she was standing on the precipice and she didn't think she was going to sleep tonight no matter what.

There was the buzzing around her that had only gotten more intense in the last few days leading to this, and yet it felt… somehow different than she'd imagined.

Different, in a good way, but in a way that was hard to explain, even to herself. Which in and of itself felt foreign to her.

The office that had served as her primary campaign base for the last year was milling with people, and she watched them as she tapped her fingers on the edge of her desk, only separated by the main room of her campaign quarters by a glass wall, before light brown eyes fell to her desk, running over the pictures there, which somehow only seemed to magnify this buzzing energy.

She paused, though, on the picture of her grandmother.

It wasn't one of her private, family photos. Not one of her on a holiday or at her wedding to Sutton or sitting with her daughters; those were at her home.

For her campaign office, she'd chosen and framed the picture of her grandmother that had been taken when Elizabeth had become the Senator of Virginia in 1980. It had happened before Charlotte had been born, her grandmother in the portrait was younger than Charlotte could remember her being in her own memory.

She would recognize the way she *looked*, anywhere, though.

It was the look in her eyes as she stood in the office Charlotte could remember well; her eyes sharp, with her arms folded over her chest, a small smile just playing at the corners of her mouth. Challenging and knowing all at once. Like everyone else in the world was just a pawn to be played in her endgame.

"This is it," she murmured, reaching out to brush her fingertips over the top of the picture frame. "Everything you did for me, everything you taught me… tonight is it."

Because tonight was the night of the election she'd been waiting for, for her whole life.

The plan she'd formulated when she'd been barely in high school, painstakingly repurposed and revised for years, under the tutelage of her grandmother. With the input of her trusted family members and friends.

Put into practice into this life she'd built with Sutton.

This election against Dylan Becker, a war "hero" and the very antithesis of who *she* was and what she stood for and what she wanted for the future of this country, had been an uphill battle from the start.

The past two years had been a thrilling and stressful test in her endurance. Using all of the skills she'd learned, taught herself, and cultivated in her fifty years, until everything had been stretched thin.

"Thank you for everything," she whispered, lightly running her thumb down the silhouette of her grandmother in the picture frame. "I'll make you proud." She promised, conviction in her tone only a fraction of what she felt inside.

No matter what the outcome of the election was, she vowed. She didn't want to face the chance that this wouldn't work out the way she'd always planned, despite it being a very real possibility.

Her lips tugged into an unstoppable smile, though, as she slid her gaze to the photographs of her daughters, perched next to her grandmother.

Madelyn grinning brightly at the camera, a headband neatly threaded through red hair, and a hand on her hip with the other slung over her little sister's shoulders, and Ellie's smile smaller, more reserved, her two front teeth missing while her dark hair was a little rumpled from having been playing before Sutton had snapped the picture.

Her daughters, who she could have lined the office with pictures of, and she wouldn't be able to see enough of their faces. Madelyn's thoughtful head tilt, and Ellie's natural pout… she looked up and out of her office, easily seeking them out in the crowd.

She didn't know when or how that happened in the last years, but sometimes she felt like she could zone in on them in the world's largest crowd. It was getting late, but she and Sutton had agreed to let both of them miss their bedtime tonight, to be here the moment everything would change.

It was their future too, after all, and Charlotte's stomach rolled in that uncontrollable feeling of anticipation and excitement, the weight of what was surmounting in front of them making the air feel thicker by the moment. Madelyn sat on the edge of one desk, laughing heartily at something Regan was saying, while Caleb milled around with Ellie piggybacking onto him like a koala.

Her girls. Her girls who she hadn't failed, hadn't damaged, who somehow became twin lights in her life in a way that she'd never imagined. Who she'd woken up to this morning as they'd both climbed into her bed and wrapped her into a tight hug, with Madelyn proclaiming, *"I can't wait 'til you win!"*

She'd laughed then, filled with the need to at the very least be powerful enough to protect her from any of the negativity that her campaign could have brought to her family's doorstep.

And she'd done that, she thought, with a nod at herself, smoothing her hands down the sides of her dress. There'd been a lot of bumps along the way, but her family was unscathed.

Her *family*.

If someone had told her twenty-five years ago that this night would come and would happen like *this*, she might have laughed in their face. Certainly would have thought they were unbalanced.

And yet, out there she had a family. Not only her parents, brothers, and Dean, she listed off silently, her eyes seeking them out in the crowd.

But her own daughters, too.

Regan, who'd joined and effectively managed her communications team in a last minute need. A woman whose company she'd hardly managed to be in who she now trusted as much as she trusted anyone who wasn't her wife.

The Spencer family, all of whom were out there for the night, a group who had become brothers and sisters that she'd never asked for, who were never afraid to tell her their thoughts, but who always showed up no matter what.

And…

Her gaze fell to the final picture. One that had been taken of Sutton on her last book tour two years ago. Her wife was tired from having taken a mini-tour – it had lasted only one month compared to the three month tour her editor had wanted her to take following the booming success of the final book in her trilogy.

The Woman in the Window had outsold even the first of her novels, had been the bestselling novel for consecutive months, and Charlotte couldn't have been prouder if she *tried*. She'd adjusted her schedule even before Sutton could possibly ask if she thought she should go on the tour.

She'd been exhausted, but she'd been luminous when she'd read selections from the novel and answered questions from the crowd. And the picture in question had been snapped at the perfect moment in time. Just as Sutton had realized that Charlotte had brought the girls to surprise her on her last stop.

It was sheer joy that was captured in that moment, she knew, as she sighed lightly, happily, staring at the picture with warmth settling low in her stomach.

She'd had a plan her entire life and somehow that plan had been completely reworked and reimagined but had still brought her to this night. To this reality that felt better than any dream she'd had in the past.

Her eyes skated over Sutton's picture again, biting her lip as something seemed to shift deep in her chest. Like a knowledge that settled over her, blanketing her with a certainty in that moment.

With that in mind, she pushed herself off of where she'd settled against her desk minutes ago to take a moment for herself. A quick glance at the clock informed her that she had less than ten minutes before the election was officially called.

And she needed to see her wife before that happened.

She smoothed her hands over the sides of her dress and drew in a deep breath as she reached the door, gathering herself before she strode back into the fray.

The second the office door was opened, she was pulled back into the energy of the night. The people who she trusted more than anything – her friends, her family – and the employees she'd trusted with her life's work, with her campaign, milled about in nervous but excited anticipation that permeated the air, silent amongst the chatter and background music.

Some sat at desks, others stood near the refreshments that had been restocked after the big dinner had been delivered hours ago. But most everyone stood across the office in a large group, where the nervous energy seemed to make everyone restless as they all stared at the same thing. The large television screens mounted to the far wall that were all broadcasting as the votes were counted, her picture and Becker's both on opposite corners of each screen, with a panel of anchors volleying back and forth as the climbing tallies were projected.

The sight of it, of those votes continuing to trickle in for these final moments, clinched up the urgent feeling inside of her. The race was going to be close and would mean more to the country than she could let herself focus on at this moment.

At this moment when she knew she'd put all of her strategy and energy and effort already into this election and could no longer do anything but wait with everyone else to see what the final vote would be.

She'd spent much of the evening pacing in front of those screens with everyone else, until she'd had to take a minute to gather her thoughts by herself. Well, she thought wryly, she'd been pacing there, her shoulders – and entire body coiled and tense – until Sutton had murmured in her ear that she should take a minute.

And her wife, unsurprisingly, had been right.

But now that Charlotte had taken that minute, she felt like she was in her own race against the clock. She needed a minute with Sutton before their lives changed forever. A moment alone.

Her eyes fell on Sutton, zeroing in on her, on the waterfall of red hair that fell over her shoulders, revealed by the sleeveless cut of her dress. Her wife might have suggested Charlotte take a moment but there she stood herself. Her hands wringing in front of her as her eyes were glued to the screen that would announce in moments whether or not Charlotte won.

She slipped through the crowd, working through the people until she made it to Sutton. Who was positively vibrating in front of her, a bright smile taking over her features as soon as she realized it was Charlotte at her side.

Before she could say anything over the din of the crowd, though, Charlotte got on her tiptoes to murmur into her ear, "Come with me, darling."

Her hand curled around Sutton's naturally, not needing to look to see where exactly her wife's hand would be as she pulled back. Her skin was soft and warm under Charlotte's palm and the energy that took up the office seemed to sizzle around them, as she tugged slightly, leading Sutton out of the room.

She drew her away from the screens, away from the people and into the hallway. It was only there that she managed to take a deep breath, when the heavy wooden doors closed behind them.

And, of course, there was this niggling part of her – a demanding part really – that would probably never go away.

A part of her that she wasn't sure if she'd been born with or if it had been simply embedded into her when she was so young that she couldn't imagine who she would be without it. That was yelling at her that her life was on the line tonight, and that line was getting shorter. That she should be with everyone else inside, staring at the numbers until it was clear whether or not she'd achieved everything she'd worked to accomplish for so long.

It was that determined, motivated part of her that would not be tempered by anything, not even herself at times, that sounded like an amalgamation of both her grandmother and herself. The part of her that thirsted and burned and didn't want to sleep at night because there was more to do in a day.

It was the part of her she'd thought would be what determined who she was for the longest time.

But an even bigger part of her demanded that she stay right here, where she was, shut away from the world she so actively fought to carve a place into. A part of her that she couldn't have imagined even existed when she'd been younger.

A part of her that had seemed to only bloom and grow when Sutton had entered her life, a part of her that had felt like the most terrifying, life changing leap to take, but imagining her life without this part of her now made her feel bereft.

The woman in front of her was the one she'd met twenty-two years ago with an errant message on a dating app, who had tangled her up in that incredibly appealing combination of boldness and unassumingness.

She could still picture the way Sutton looked on the first day they'd met at Topped Off, the flush on her cheeks and the exact timbre of her voice.

The one who'd made her fall in love somewhere between drinking coffee and stroking her hair back when she was sick and making her laugh over late movie nights.

She didn't think she would ever be able to get over the ease with which Sutton situated herself into her life, without Charlotte even realizing it had happened.

The one who'd confessed her love for her tearfully in a café.

The one who had packed a picnic the day after her brother's wedding and had brought Charlotte to an alcove in the woods behind her parents' house, looking adorably pleased with herself.

"I figured, um, this could be our first official date," she'd said, a blush adorning her cheeks, charming Charlotte utterly and completely. "Because, you know, we're together now and you said you haven't had an official date, because of – well. Everything."

The one who'd been there with her, squeezing her hand, during her first congressional election.

She'd knocked down all of Charlotte's walls and restored them so that they'd fit the both of them. She was the one who had been there with her through everything. She was the one who made her laugh so hard she cried, who held her when she truly needed to cry. They'd brought life into this world, they'd lost family members, and it was – it was Sutton who was there at the beginning and end of everything.

The same woman and yet completely different after so many years, and Charlotte never thought she'd grow *with* someone like this, but here they were.

It wasn't the first time that the magnitude of all she felt for Sutton took her breath away and made her knees feel weak, but something about this moment made her feel so reverent as she tracked her eyes over Sutton's face.

Twenty-two years, and her wife was more beautiful than the first time she'd seen her, she thought, as she felt her heart pound in her chest.

Sutton's blue eyes were bright, running over Charlotte's face in confusion, as she asked, "Where are we going, love? We're just about to see that you won!"

"I'd spent so much of my life with this election, with tonight, meaning so much," the words felt so heavy with truth as they left her. "With this election, this night, being this make or break moment for my entire *life*." This was in her blood, this was her life's work, and nothing was ever going to change that.

But…

Sutton's forehead furrowed with concern evident all over her features as her eyes searched Charlotte's, even as a gentle, comforting grin tugged softly at those soft lips. "I know. Tonight is everything." She nodded with her words, even as she reached out to take Charlotte's other hand in hers.

She gripped her wife's hands, squeezing them with this urgency she felt inside. "No," she breathed out on a surprised laugh. "It's actually not."

That had been the realization, the one that felt like a stark slap in the face, the one that had stolen her breath right from her chest.

"Charlotte, what are you saying? Because we have hundreds of people on the other side of that door. Our girls, our friends and family, the top team who worked on your campaign, and the news is almost here." Sutton shook her head slightly, amused exasperation coloring her tone.

She leaned a bit closer, the smell of her subtle perfume that Charlotte knew anywhere enveloping them as she carefully searched over Charlotte's features. "Are you all right?" It was like the same buzz Charlotte had felt all night was also wound tightly around Sutton, and she *loved* her so much for it.

For all of it.

"I know you haven't gotten much sleep lately, maybe –" The worry in Sutton's voice grew bit by bit as she used her hold on Charlotte's hands to pull her closer, then traced her hand up to tilt Charlotte up by the chin.

She let her, moving easily with her wife's touch, even as she shook her head to cut her off. "No, I mean, it *is* important, of course. This election is so important, darling, for me. And you, and our family, and the future of our country. And I want it so badly I can taste it." She wanted it so badly, her stomach hadn't settled for days as they'd drawn closer to the election.

But that was just it.

She could lose this election. It wouldn't be out of the realm of possibility, despite how much everything inside of her revolted against the idea. She took everything that her grandmother had taught her, all of the lessons she'd learned herself, all of the wisdom and strength and support from her wife, and had turned it into a campaign that was so strong, it had been commended by many experts in the field.

But there was no guarantee.

There was so much riding on this and if she lost she would be devastated, it was true. If she lost this, she would shed actual tears. She would need to be consoled by her wife, have to take considerable time to reframe her plans and her future. That was a truth that was ingrained into her bones.

Sutton simply nodded softly, her thumb gentle as she stroked at Charlotte's cheek, and she easily turned into the feeling, appreciating Sutton's patience as she waited for Charlotte to continue.

"I just need you to know, darling, that I have spent my entire life believing that if there is such a thing as destiny, that this is mine. To become the President, to change the world. And being with you strengthened that, in a way, because you make me stronger." She bit at her lip, able to see the way her words brought that warm, loving flush to Sutton's cheeks.

"But I…" She took in a deep, shaking breath, feeling like the world around her was shifting. "I need you to know that more than anything, *you* are what made this possible." She searched Sutton's eyes. "Maybe I would have been President no matter what, but if I didn't have you here to do it with me, my life wouldn't be full."

She swallowed hard, pressing closer to Sutton, wanting to feel her as she whispered, "I don't know if there's a destiny, but I know that if there is, you're mine."

She knew it in her bones. If she lost this election, her life would be altered but it would not be over. There would be a new election, one day, there would be another chance in the future to regroup for.

If she lost Sutton somehow, it would not be so simple as to say there would be another day. A life without winning this election was still full of possibility, of more to come. A life without Sutton would be nothing.

Sutton's hands slid to her waist, and she sighed into her mouth, her hands curling over Sutton's shoulders instinctively as she moved onto her tiptoes to be even closer.

She could feel the way Sutton's heartbeat skipped as Charlotte pulled her even closer and she knew her own mirrored it, as she nibbled at her wife's bottom lip, reveling in her for a long moment. And even when she released her mouth, she didn't pull away. Couldn't pull away, not quite yet.

Sutton shifted, leaning her temple against Charlotte's while her hands stroked at her hips and even though her dress, she felt herself shiver even as she leaned into her wife's warmth.

"I think I've known you were my destiny since the moment I saw your picture," Sutton whispered, her voice thick with emotion. Charlotte's eyes fluttered closed at the way her words washed over her, the way they made everything inside of Charlotte feel better, fuller.

The way Sutton herself made Charlotte's life feel better and fuller.

And for a few moments, they stayed there in the quiet hallway filled with only them – their voices, their emotions, just to be together for a few moments before their lives would change forever – when on the other side of the door, their daughters, their family, and their future were waiting for them.

She felt recharged from it, even before Sutton sighed softly into her ear and leaned away, her hands sliding to land on Charlotte's arms. "I'm happy we are having this moment to ourselves," she began, before she bit her lip, her eyes glinting in the way that delighted Charlotte down to her toes. "But I did not campaign for years to not be in that room when we finally learn that my wife is the new President of the United States."

A laugh broke from her lips, echoing in the hallway, even as she thought about the last interview she'd done, where an interviewer had asked if she was looking forward to being the most powerful woman in the world. And her first response had been to tell him he should be asking that to her wife.

"And I'm going to be right by your side when Dylan Becker has to call and concede to you. I can't wait to hear that little asshole congratulate you after everything he's done." Sutton sighed out an annoyed breath.

Becker's campaign had done dirty, trying to pull out every stop in the books to try to get voters to sway toward him. It worked for most conservatives but she'd taken the highest road possible.

Still, though, she found herself laughing, affection shooting through her. "So aggressive, darling. Where is my mild-mannered wife?"

Sutton shot her a *look* before a glint gleamed in those bright blue eyes. "I guess I've been with you long enough for you to rub off on me."

"Lucky me." She met her wife's grin with her own before she nodded to herself.

Slowly, she took a step back, missing the way Sutton felt against her, but feeling readier now. Ready for whatever their future was going to show them. The tension that had coiled earlier was back now, as there was a blast of sound – shouting – from inside.

It was time.

She didn't let go of Sutton's hand, though, even as they started walking, wanting the connection with her. "Are you ready? Everything is going to change."

Sutton's hand squeezed back, blue eyes searching hers for a long moment, nothing but certainty reflecting back. "I'm ready for anything with you."

***

Time Magazine || Person of the Year
Charlotte Thompson: The Power of a Legacy
Dec. 30 2044

As Thompson's first term of presidency comes to an end, it would be impossible to ignore the impact she's had on this country. With a consistently record-breaking approval rating, regularly holding firm at 85, the country has seen record lows of unemployment as the economy has soared. With a notably deft-hand at managing foreign affairs, the domestic prosperity in terms of prison and healthcare reform has been significant.

In her own right, Sutton Thompson's very hands-on work in terms of educational support and making strides toward closing the discrepancy in social stratification has been notable. See page 10 for more details on current plans in place.

Seen as a beacon of hope for some and pillars of strength for others, the couple's legacy and success has already made a mark. Already hailed by many as a Golden Age for this country, we look forward to what comes next.

Other books by Haley Cass

Those Who Wait

Sutton Spencer's ideas for her life were fairly simple: finish graduate school and fall in love. It would be a lot simpler if she could pinpoint exactly what she should do when she graduates in less than a year. Oh, and if she could figure out how to talk to a woman without feeling like a total mess, that would be great too.

Charlotte Thompson is very much the opposite. She's always had clear steps outlining her path to success with no time or inclination for romance. Her burgeoning career in politics means everything to her and she's not willing to compromise it for something as insignificant as love. Fleeting, casual, and discreet worked perfectly fine.

When they meet through a dating app, it's immediately clear that they aren't suited for anything more than friendship. Right?

When You Least Expect It

Caroline Parker knows three things to be true. First, she is going to be Boston's most sought after divorce attorney by thirty-five. Second, given how terrible her romantic track record is, falling in love isn't in the cards for her. And third, Christmas only brings her bad luck - being broken up with not once, not twice, but three times during the holidays is proof enough of that.

When she runs into Hannah Dalton on Christmas Eve, she has no reason to believe her luck will change. After all, though Hannah is probably the most gorgeous woman she's ever seen, she's also straight. And married to Caroline's work rival. While being hired by Hannah throws her for a loop, winning a divorce case and sticking it to her ex-colleague should be enough of a thrill. But as the months slip by, bringing her closer to both Hannah and her adorable daughter Abbie, the lines between attorney and client begin to blur.

And she could have never predicted just how much she wants them to.

Better Than Expected

Hannah Dalton had a lot of expectations in her life. Growing up watching her mother struggle for everything they had, she resolved to make sure she did everything she could to make those hardships worthwhile. She would pursue the career she dreamed of, she would marry someone trustworthy and kind, and she would try to give her own daughter everything her mother gave her, only without the struggle.

She just never anticipated the order in which it could all happen or the hardships that would inevitably come to pass. But, somehow, maybe it can all work out better than expected.

A companion to the bestselling novel When You Least Expect It.

Down to A Science

Ellie Beckett's life is simple and uncomplicated; she's on track to become a leading expert in biomedical engineering, she has a pub where she feels comfortable enough to hang out multiple times a week, and, so what if she doesn't have time for… people? She doesn't need or want them.

Until she meets Mia Sharpe.

As it it turns out, maybe Ellie does want at least one person.

On the Same Page

Riley Beckett met Gianna Mäkinen – drop-dead gorgeous influencer, trilingual, daughter of world-famous models, yes, that Gianna Mäkinen – their first year at Boston University, and it changed everything for the both of them. After all, when you find the person who just gets you, nothing feels quite "the same" right?

And in the ten years since, Riley has come to depend on Gianna more than anyone else in her life. She knows Gianna just as well as she knows herself – maybe better, some days. She knows Gianna is incredibly sex-positive, she knows Gianna doesn't do romance or relationships, and she knows nothing could ever come between them.

This is what makes sense to her, all of this is status-quo. But when a holiday party mix-up sets in motion a domino effect of changes to these previously inalienable truths, Riley has to question everything she thought she knew about their relationship. What, exactly, does Gianna mean to her after all?

About the Author

Haley lives in Philadelphia with her partner, but she is originally from Massachusetts. No matter what, she is dedicated to living on the east coast, where she has a love/hate relationship with the weather extremities but would also hate to live somewhere without fall foliage. She spends most of her time watching too much television and thinking about the future. Oh, and writing.

Her mother likes to talk about the time she wrote her first story while sitting under the kitchen table for privacy. Twenty years later, she still likes to write but is slightly too tall to sit under the kitchen table.

Printed in Great Britain
by Amazon